Leaders & L

The Legends
of Lake on
the Mountain

An Early Adventure of
JOHN A. MACDONALD

With a Foreword by former
Prime Minister Brian Mulroney

By Roderick Benns

Fireside Publishing House

This book is fiction but many of the characters and events are based on real people and actual historical events.

ISBN 978-0-9812433-2-0 (pbk.)
ISBN 978-0-9812433-1-3

$12.95 CDN.

Fireside Publishing House
www.firesidepublishinghouse.com

For an Access Copyright license, visit www.accesscopyright.ca or call (toll-free) 1-800-893-5777.

Library and Archives Canada Cataloguing in Publication

Benns, Roderick, 1970-
    The legends of Lake on the Mountain : an early adventure of John A. Macdonald / by Roderick Benns ; foreword by Brian Mulroney. -- Collector's ed.

(Leaders & legacies series ; bk. 2)
ISBN 978-0-9812433-2-0

    1. Macdonald, John A. (John Alexander), 1815-1891--Childhood and youth--Juvenile fiction. I. Title. II. Series: Leaders & legacies series

PS8603.E5598L44 2010   jC813'.6   C2010-906596-4

Printed and bound in Canada by Maracle Press Ltd.

Cover art, book design and illustrations by riad

Acknowledgements

I would like to acknowledge the hard work and dedication of Joli Scheidler-Benns, an outstanding editor and partner. What a fantastic series this is becoming because of her efforts.

A special thank you and sincere note of gratitude to the Right Honourable Brian Mulroney for his time and generosity in supporting this book and series concept with his Foreword. To Arthur Milnes, Francine Collins and Robin Sears, thank you for your facilitation and support. For author-historians Richard Gwyn, Jack Granatstein and Patricia Phenix, I truly appreciate your willingness to share your names and credibility to this project.

Many people were there for me during the writing of this book with their specialized knowledge, their contacts and their enthusiasm. Thanks to Janet Kellough and Steve Campbell for their knowledge of Prince Edward County. On a related note, thanks to The Historical Archives for the County of Prince Edward. The staff was most helpful while I conducted research.

Thanks to Ted Hazen of Pennsylvania for sharing his deep knowledge of historical grist mills on both sides of the border.

Thanks to my younger brother, Captain Brad Benns, for imparting his military knowledge for key scenes in this book.

Books in the Leaders & Legacies Series

Book One
The Mystery of the Moonlight Murder:
An Early Adventure of John Diefenbaker

Book Two
The Legends of Lake on the Mountain:
An Early Adventure of John A. Macdonald

Upcoming

An Early Adventure of Paul Martin
An Early Adventure of Lester Pearson
An Early Adventure of Charles Tupper
An Early Adventure of Kim Campbell

...and more

For Brothers

For Captain Bradley E. Benns
of the Canadian Armed Forces

For Clayton, the one I never knew

"...I have fought the battle of Confederation, the battle of union, the battle of the Dominion of Canada...I know that, notwithstanding the many failings in my life, I shall have the voice of this country..."

– Prime Minister John A. Macdonald
November 3, 1873

Contents

Foreword by the
Right Honourable Brian Mulroney   *i*

1	Ghosts	21
2	The Survivor	28
3	Milling About	41
4	Darius	47
5	Treasure	56
6	The Games People Play	68
7	The Colour of Oppression	73
8	Macpherson	82
9	The Lake Serpent	86
10	The Admiral	97
11	Devil's Lake	100
12	The Lake Effect	109
13	Democracy is Coming	113
14	The Constable's Search	121
15	A Greater Good	124
16	As Mean as They Come	129
17	Lake of the Gods	138
18	Exodus	141
19	Manifest Destiny	150
20	'That Lake's No Good'	155
21	The Leviathan	158
22	Battles are Won in the Mind	163
23	Of Monsters and Men	169
24	A Matter of Perspective	177
25	Imagine What we Could Become	182
26	The Truth of it All	192

Fiction or fact?   205

Late August, 1828
in Stone Mills, Upper Canada
(known today as Glenora, in
Prince Edward County, Ontario)

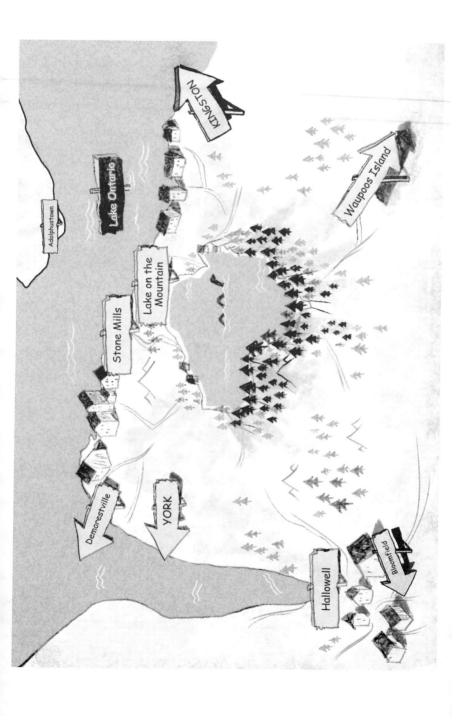

Foreword

by

The Right Honourable M. Brian Mulroney

18th Prime Minister of Canada

Sir John A. Macdonald never forgot what it was like to be a child. Shortly before his death in 1891 he took the time to answer a letter from a young girl in Ontario's Prince Edward County, the place where he had spent many of his childhood years. The girl told the Prime Minister that she had previously written to a young man and that her letter had not been answered.

"My dear little Friend," John A. wrote back, "…I think it was mean of that young fellow not to answer your letter. You see, I have been longer in the world than he, and know more than he does what is due to young ladies. I send you a dollar note with which pray buy some small keepsake to remember me by."

On the same winter that Sir John A. and the girl had their exchange of letters Macdonald faced Canadians in an election for the final time. As cold winter winds chilled his weary bones, the 76-year-old John A. travelled the young country speaking in person to Canadians a final time. He was greeted by the same shout wherever he went. "Sir John," people yelled in respect and affection, "you'll never die."

As we can see from books like this Leaders & Legacies series volume on Sir John A. that you are about to read, the Canadians who shouted that prophecy more than one hundred years ago were correct. Sir John A. Macdonald's life and legacy continues to stir and inspire us to this very day. And because, in part, of books like The Legends of Lake on the Mountain: *An Early Adventure of John A. Macdonald*, he remains with us still.

One of my fondest memories of my own service as Prime Minister of Canada was a trip to Kingston, the Canadian home of Sir John A., which I took on June 6, 1991. It was the one hundredth anniversary of Sir John A's death. At the Macdonald family plot at historic Cataraqui Cemetery it was my honour to represent all Canadians that day in paying respect to the memory of our greatest Prime Minister.

As they do every year on that date, Kingstonians had gathered in great numbers at the cemetery. People from all walks of life and all political persuasions were united in paying tribute to Canada's Father of Confederation.

I returned to my duties in Ottawa energized by my visit to Kingston and inspired again by Sir John A's example and story.

Like all Prime Ministers, I began my life-long love of books and reading during my childhood. As a class project in Grade 5 in Baie Comeau, my teacher required me and my fellow students to keep a daily diary for one term. My late mother, Irene Mulroney – just as I suspect your own parents have done – kept my diary long after I'd forgotten it. Only recently, I reviewed this diary as I was writing my Memoirs.

When Roderick Benns first approached me about contributing this Foreword to his adventure book about our first Prime Minister, I immediately thought of one of the diary passages I had written in Baie Comeau more than 60 years ago and only recently read again.

"Yesterday I finished my story-book about Buddy and the G-Man mystery," I wrote on October 10, 1947. "It was a very good book and I liked it very much."

Written by legendary children's author Howard Garis, Buddy and the G-Man Mystery or, a Boy and a Strange Cipher, was first published in 1944. Like countless other young people across North America, I spent hours enthralled by that adventure story. Decades later, I can recall how the book and so many like it I read after my frequent visits to the town library inspired me and stirred my imagination.

In addition to serving as Prime Minister, John A and I had something else in common – we have both lost a brother. I was always struck by the fact that even late in life John A. had never forgotten his brother, even recording his death in the family's memorandum book where, for some reason, it had been left out.

My brother – who was also named John – sadly passed away shortly after he was born. While I never knew him I often wonder what it would have been like to have had an older sibling. I wonder about the kind of person he might have been. I wonder how our lives might have been shaped by one another.

Prime Ministers are human beings, as the Leaders & Legacies series shows through storytelling. They suffer devastating personal tragedies, sacrifice their personal freedom, and agonize over the issues that might threaten their beloved country. They do this on behalf of all Canadians. But they persevere. If I were to take on the role of mentor for even a brief moment, I would say to any young person reading, persevere. Persist as John A Macdonald did. Find your own unique way to serve your family, community or country.

I am confident that young Canadians reading The Legends of Lake on the Mountain: *An Early Adventure of John A. Macdonald* will find themselves inspired and engaged like I was upon reading my first adventure novels in Baie Comeau as a boy. This wonderful story will also serve to inspire young readers to learn more about Sir John A. Macdonald and early Canada along the way.

Mr. Benns and his wife, Joli, who served as editor of The Legends of Lake on the Mountain: *An Early Adventure of John A. Macdonald*, are to be congratulated for all the work they have done in bringing this important book to fruition.

The Right Honourable
M. Brian Mulroney
18th Prime Minister of Canada
Montreal, Quebec
September 2010

Chapter 1

Ghosts

Here lies John A. Macdonald.
Born January 11, 1815 in Glasgow, Scotland.
Died August 20, 1828, in Stone Mills, Upper Canada.
A clever boy – but just not clever enough.

John considered how his tombstone would read as he sweated underneath Owen Boggart's armpit. Although he had escaped the heavy-set man-child and his meaty fists all summer, John had finally pushed his luck too far as Owen dragged him across the ground.

Owen was not so inclined to win spelling bees or solve complex sums in his head. What the fourteen-year-old was known for was his effectiveness at wreaking vengeance – especially on those who might be poking fun at him.

Lanky and far lighter than his adversary, John was surprised to find himself being dragged to the stone flour mill. It was John's father, Hugh Macdonald, who ran it. He pictured the overweight boy crushing him into flour. The Macdonald's house was only thirty feet away, but no one was outside to hear the commotion.

John saw another perfect sunset washing across the bay, bathing the village in a painter's light. He was sorry he had to see it through the filter of Owen's armpit. Stone Mills was a small, bustling community that sat on the edge of the Bay of Quinte, a magnificent collection of long, watery fingers that stretched out into Lake Ontario. Not only did the village sit along the bay, supporting the Macdonald's flour mill and other businesses, it also rested at the bottom of a spectacular, forested, flat-topped hill nearly two-hundred-feet high. The locals just called it a mountain.

On top of the flattened mountain was a small, mysterious lake, which John desperately hoped he would see again, if he survived this ordeal. There was nothing he loved more than to explore its twisted shoreline. John had even heard rumours lately that there had been sightings of something strange in the lake – something incredible.

The mill grew closer.

Perhaps Father was still working at the mill?

John's silent question was answered by Owen, as if he could pluck it out of his head and spit it back at him.

"Your father's not there. You think I'm stupid?"

asked Owen.

John bit his tongue. He was often amused by such obvious questions. As the hot breath of the furious boy scorched the back of his neck John kicked and thrashed in vain. He realized the mill would have recently shut down and his father would be putting in time helping the Robinson's with their new barn, as he had been doing all week.

The sun winked out of view as they entered the main floor of the three-level mill. John hoped to see one of his father's employees still working. Only the silent millstones stared back at him. He could hear the lull of the waterfall behind the mill, which powered every-thing. John listened for sounds from the basement where the meal bins were located but didn't hear any-one there, either. Finally, he craned his neck upwards in case anyone was still in the grain storage area of the attic. No sound. No one.

"You better not scream, Johnny. If you do, you'll only make things worse for yourself."

Owen was bold enough to humiliate John on his own property. In fact, he was even bold enough to call him 'Johnny.'

"Listen," said John, "Obviously there is some clear misunderstanding. What is it exactly that you think I've done?"

The boy grunted. "You know what you did. You and

George put a dead squirrel in my hat when I had it off at the bay yesterday. And now yer gonna get what you deserve – and George is next."

John, despite being folded underneath Owen's unpleasantly-scented armpit, managed to pop his curly-haired head out and feign shock. "Now what would give you the impression that George and I would do such a thing?"

"Hilda Scott saw you both do it." With that, Owen head-locked John again and continued dragging the slimmer boy toward a corner of the large, open room.

"Hilda Scott!" John snorted. "You know you should never take the word of a Scot."

John began to sweat more as he realized his humour wasn't going to secure his escape this time. It was time to change tactics. "You're right. It was a dastardly prank," said John. "Perhaps I could help you in school with your worst subjects?" John wondered if that would mean 'everything,' but didn't say so.

"You should know I don't go to school anymore, Johnny. Not that I ever did with you anyway. Not everyone gets to go to a fancy grammar school in Kingston. Some of us just make do with what's here."

Owen tightened his grip on John's neck.

"You show up in the summer here at Stone Mills, thinking yer something special," Owen said. His fleshy face was heated. "Well this summer, maybe you'll figure out yer nothing special…"

The sound of voices outside in the distance prompted Owen to release his grip slightly. John wondered if he should try to break free and run as Owen jerked his round face toward the noise. The powerful boy forced John up against a huge pile of flour sacks that were sitting in the corner. One of the sacks was torn open, already oozing ground white flour.

The thickset boy shoved one of his paws in swiftly and scooped a generous amount of flour. He rubbed it all over John's face and curly locks of dark hair until every inch of his hair and face were covered in dusty, white flour. John gasped and coughed as some went up his nose and in his mouth. With a satisfied smirk, Owen shoved his instant ghost to the ground.

"Yer lucky that's all you got, Johnny," spat the giant boy. And without another word Owen hulked away from the mill, running east along a dirt path, wiping his white hand on his shirt as he ran. John watched him go from a small window in the mill, blinking flour from his sweating eyelids. When he felt he was out of view, John punched the air with his fist in glee and let out a long whoop.

He had survived Owen Boggart! John mentally dismantled the tombstone he had created earlier, then burst from the darkened doorway. He ran west and at the last second, John locked eyes with a young boy, perhaps four-years-old, who was out walking with his grandfather. The boy opened his mouth and screamed at the ghostly image charging toward him. The flour-covered John began to scream because he thought Owen must be behind him. John barrelled the young boy over, tripping himself along the way.

"Dang fool!" he heard the older man yell.

"Apologies!" hollered John, who had already picked himself up and scurried along the shore. His bare feet splashed along the bay, forcing warm sand between his toes. He fled to the very edge of Stone Mills, laughing so hard he had to clear tears from his eyes as he ran.

The more he ran, the more he thought how much the young boy had reminded him of his younger brother, little James, who had died at age five. John remembered how James had followed him everywhere, in the way little brothers do, even though John had only been seven.

As the sunset bled across the bay, John collapsed in a ghostly heap on the shoreline. Memories of the tavern in Kingston flooded his mind and he pressed his palms to his eyes. His tears of laughter had already turned to tears for the cruel death of his little brother.

He rolled over onto his knees and looked into the water at his smeared, white features and bit into his lip. As much as he could escape the Owen Boggart's of the world, there was one thing John believed he would never be free from – knowing that it was his fault his little brother was murdered.

As the waves shifted, he touched the side of his face. John slid his hands beneath the water and let the flawed image strain between his fingers.

The trembling water soon settled. Once again, the ghost had returned.

Chapter 2

The Survivor

Anson Rightmyer was a survivor. Sixteen years ago he had survived the War of 1812 in dramatic fashion during his first outing as a soldier. As a sweaty palmed, twenty-two-year-old scarecrow, he had hidden in a ditch, crouched down with seven other British soldiers and three Indians.

As he stood to take his first shot of the war an American infantryman shot a bullet into his head. Of course, it had only nicked the top of his skull, giving him a lifetime of bad haircuts. But he had made it, hadn't he?

He felt his unusual, double-hair part as he walked, one natural, the other bullet-made. Touching this area several times a day helped him remember what he could get through. The strange sounds he had heard coming from the forest beside his own farm this evening didn't scare a man like Anson Rightmyer as much as peak his curiosity. The woods were thick and uninviting here, even for hunters. He thought he had heard a number of voices but who could be mucking about so deeply in the forest? Maybe he'd hang right and go to the edge of the lake.

After the war, when he and his wife Mary Ann first broke land to farm on top of Lake on the Mountain, they had almost died that first winter. The crop had been so poor they had nearly starved. But with a little begging and borrowing from established neighbours and lots of creative cooking from Mary Ann, they had made it. God rest her soul, she had made sure of that.

Last spring Mary Ann caught the consumption and couldn't hang on. After Mary Ann's death, Anson lost his baby finger on his left hand from a saw mill accident. Then he stumbled and fell into a ravine six months ago and sprained his ankle. Two weeks ago, he had thrown up from eating bear meat he had tried to save for too long. As he walked, he pondered another possibility; maybe he was only a survivor with Mary Ann? Maybe he couldn't sense the shape of his life without her.

Anson used both of his slim, white arms in front of him to shove back the thick bush. Disturbed bugs flew into his mouth and he hacked and spit until they expelled. He stumbled from the outskirts of the forest to the edge of the small, mysterious lake. Lake on the Mountain stared back at him in the twilight and he sighed, realizing he would have no luck in the diminished light. As he watched the lake, he saw something break the surface of the water. A dark hump rose up then dipped below again. Another hump, right behind it, took its place.

"What the…"

Then a long, serpent-like neck broke through the surface and turned towards Anson. In his petrified state – and just before he was about to scream – he felt a cold, strong hand clamp over his mouth.

***

"Moll!" John called in a hushed voice. He could see his eldest sister in the semi-darkness, fetching water from their well. Her porcelain-like features were muted by twilight.

"John, where have you been?" Moll asked. "And what happened to you?"

John could see she was eyeing his hair and face. He had tried to clean up at the bay, but he was bound to have missed some flour.

"Let's just say Owen Boggart wasn't too happy with me."

"Well, now Mother isn't, either," said Moll, finishing her task. She drew a full pail of water from the well. At fourteen-years-old, Moll was a year older than John. When John wanted to talk about something or play chess, he turned to Moll. When he wanted to play out-side or even roughhouse, he turned to his younger sister, Lou. Although Lou played chess, too, Moll offered more of a challenge, since she was older.

John sighed. "Alright, but never mind that for a second. Did you hear anything new about the sightings in the lake?"

Moll turned with the full pail and set it down. "No – but I think Father might know more. I heard a few people talking to him today at the mill about it when I was walking by. He isn't home yet."

John nodded and looked at the front door. "Guess I have to go in?"

"Sooner or later," said Moll. She grabbed her bucket and John reluctantly followed.

Helen Macdonald, their mother, was cleaning the kitchen when they walked in. She met him with a stern scowl.

"I declare, you nearly scared the new Clancy boy half to death, John Macdonald!"

John sat with his head in his hands on a thick wooden bench at the kitchen table. He watched the stuttering oil lamp melt the late evening darkness away. His mother's tall frame cast over-sized shadows on the wall behind her. John knew his father, Hugh Macdonald, would soon trudge through the door – tired and talkative.

"That boy's grandfather was just here complaining

about your scandalous behaviour. The poor lad will likely have nightmares."

John pictured the young boy who had reminded him so much of his younger brother. It had been five years and no one ever talked about James.

Ever.

John always got the impression that remembering James was somehow wrong.

"Don't you have anything to say?" his mother demanded. "If not, that'd be a first, wouldn't it?"

John stuttered a few words but then halted and just sighed.

"You – looking like some sort of common ruffian – and knocking people over. I didn't raise you to be some kind of heathen, did I? What were you thinking?"

John held up his hands in exasperation at the long kitchen table. A glance at a small, hanging mirror on his way in told him his face was clean but he had streaks of white flour in his mop-like hair which had artificially aged him.

"I'm sorry, Mother. I was trying to escape Owen Boggart – he dunked my head in the flour and I was just trying to get away."

"Hmmph. Now why would that boy do such a thing? You must have done something to deserve it."

Helen Macdonald was nobody's fool – even when it came to her own children. She knew that John

Macdonald – as proud as she was of him for his clever brain – had something of the living mischief in him.

"Mother!" replied John, looking astonished. "George and I, knowing what an animal lover Owen Boggart is, merely left a squirrel in his care – thinking he would take good care of it."

Her eyes narrowed as her looming shadow followed her. "And this squirrel, it was the alive kind?" As a large-boned woman, she even looked down upon John's father.

"Mother, all I can say is that I saw some movement from the squirrel when we left it for him." John recalled yesterday's windy day and the fur of the dead squirrel blowing about. Technically, the squirrel was moving. He hoped his mother would stop questioning him.

Just then John heard the main door creak. Hugh Macdonald opened the door and mumbled hello but immediately headed to the wash basin to soak his face and wash his hands. As he did so, Helen caught him up on John's 'trouble' as she called it.

John's father sat down opposite of his only son. He rubbed his head with both hands like he always did after work. Then he rubbed his hands lower toward his eyes and rubbed some more. Hugh blinked away the stars he had created in front of his vision and John could not help but notice his large moustache was now askew.

Helen set a cup of hot tea in front of her husband. He

nodded his thanks.

"I'm not going to say anything more about this, John, because it sounds like your mother has dealt with it. But you stay out of the mill after hours, you hear? We can't afford to have any equipment broken. And I'll say something else..."

John bit his tongue. *I thought you weren't going to say anything...*

"We don't need any trouble from any of the farming families, you hear?" Hugh slurped his steaming tea.

"But Father, they... "

Hugh raised his hand to cut him off. "Do you know how important this time of year is for us?"

John sensed the shift in tone from his father – this would probably be the speech about milling and farming existing in partnership.

"You should know by now that milling and farming exist in partnership," said Hugh.

I knew it.

"..and that means the farmer expects quick and reliable service from us. It's late August now and we're just getting started with the harvest. We can't be giving them any reasons to take their wheat elsewhere or ship it off to some other place."

"Yes, Father."

Helen chimed in. "Just wait 'til September rolls around if you think this is busy. While we pay for you to be able to attend school, this place will be packed with farm folks. You won't see all that in Kingston, though."

John bit his tongue. On the one hand, his parents sent him to Kingston to go to a proper school for the good of the whole family. They expected him to make something of himself. On the other hand, his parents always pointed out how much he was away, as if he was missing out on real work.

A scuffle from John's sisters' room could be heard, before ten-year-old Louisa – who was Lou to everyone – fell half out into the main room.

"Oh, hello Father," Lou said. She said it as if it was perfectly natural to fall out of one's room. Her dark hair fell about her shoulders and she picked herself up, reclaiming her stern look, which was her most natural one.

"There's my Lou!" said Hugh, motioning for a hug. Lou approached smiling, casting a glance toward her older brother.

"Father," said Lou, "Moll was just wondering if you heard any news about the...well, that is, about the thing in the lake?"

"Louisa!" said Moll, exiting from their bedroom. No one called Lou by her real name unless they were angry with her. "I did not wonder – it was you!"

Hugh laughed while John's ears perked up. He

wanted to know everything about any lake incident, too. Perhaps he and George could visit there tomorrow.

"If by news of the lake you mean more 'creature sightings' then no – no more news," said Hugh. "In other words, Whisky Wilson hasn't likely been drinking as much – at least for today."

'Whisky Wilson' was actually Walt Wilson, though no one ever called him that. As his father had explained it, late yesterday afternoon Whisky had run into the centre of the village to say he had just seen a serpent with two great humps swimming in the lake. He had even told Constable Charles Ogden, the only real law and order presence in the area. However, even as Whisky told his story his left hand gripped the neck of a jug – likely whisky – and only a few people were willing to listen to him for long.

As manager of the mill, Hugh Macdonald was the centre of the town and he didn't miss many rumours. He had a gift for the gab and people tended to open up to him naturally.

"The Mohawk believe the lake is haunted," said John. "Maybe it is."

"Well, that's nonsense," said Hugh. "Listen, haunted lakes are bad for business in case anyone here hasn't thought of that. We run a flour mill the last time I checked. It's too easy to get people whipped up about nothing. We don't need to be adding to the nonsense."

Helen began adding oil to two lamps that were low. "Don't forget the colonel is coming tomorrow."

"Yay!" said John, echoed by Moll and Lou. Hugh grunted, gulping the rest of his tea down. His jovial features darkened some.

The colonel was Lieutenant Colonel Donald Macpherson, John's uncle by marriage. As a retired British officer, the colonel lived in Kingston and he and his wife, Anna, originally hosted the Macdonald's when they arrived from Scotland when John was just five-years-old. He was a veteran soldier who had fought twice against the Americans – once during the War of Independence and again in the War of 1812, sixteen years ago. John was especially close to him and saw him often during the school year in Kingston. He and the colonel would often watch the red-coated British soldiers emerge from Fort Henry to march to a military drum beat and the forlorn sounds of bagpipes. Sometimes they would even watch the great sailing ships speckle the open water of Lake Ontario.

Hugh and the colonel had a different kind of relationship though, bordering more on the adversarial.

"And now I know why he's coming, too." From his pocket he pulled out a sheet of paper and spread it out on the table.

"Not another one," Helen said. It was the second time they had seen *The Stone Mills Reformer*, a single-page news sheet that condemned the current system of government. The first one, just last month, had contained similar headlines. Helen read over his shoulder.

"Increase the Power of Elected Members. Family Compact Must Go. Responsible Government: It's Time."

She looked at Hugh. "Who's printing these?"

Hugh scoffed. "I wouldn't know – but it's something more that's bad for business, that's what it is." John wondered about the news sheet, too. Criticizing the government so strongly seemed overly harsh – something Americans were more inclined to do.

"Alright, to bed with you three," said Helen. "John, you be available to your father tomorrow morning when the wagons start arriving with wheat. You can help with all the unloading."

John drooped. "But Mother, what if George shows up? He said he might be able to come by tomorrow morning." He had envisioned skipping stones across the bay and maybe exploring the lake for Whisky Wilson's humped creature.

"Good for George," said Helen. "That's one more pair of hands that can help out."

John could feel his mother's eyes remaining on him. He wilted further to see if he could change her mind.

"Listen," said Helen, softening. "We know you'll soon be going off to Kingston. You'll get some extra time to have fun."

Hugh raised an eyebrow at his wife but didn't say anything.

"But that doesn't mean you get to do as you please whenever you want, understood?"

"Yes, of course, Mother."

John retired to his bedroom for the night as did Moll and Lou. He lit his oil lamp for the few minutes that were allowed to get settled. Having it on too long would be considered a waste of fuel, so he didn't linger.

Before he blew it out, John reached for his carving knife and felt the handle mould to his palm. Under his blanket he found a stick he had been whittling. John made extra care to whittle in silence in the darkness while he thought about a creature roaming the depths of Lake on the Mountain. He had heard the Mohawk legends since they first arrived in the area. But this was the first time someone had reported anything, even if it was Whisky Wilson.

The gentle sounds of the waterfall behind the mill were comforting. John could picture it careening down the mountain from the mysterious lake. The water gathered into a long, wooden raceway into a thick, white, watery thread as it continuously pounded into the grist mill's wheel.

His parents were talking in low voices, but John had learned to hear through their murmurs and over the sounds of the falling water. He stopped whittling. He didn't want to miss anything.

"...it makes no sense...even if he's not happy about the news sheet what's he going to do?" said Hugh. "He doesn't work for the Tories...just an old man who's always voted Tory."

Hugh's voice hummed across the sitting area. John couldn't hear what his mother replied. He slid his knife and stick underneath his bed and pulled the blanket over his shoulder. With the colonel coming, John wondered if he'd have to go back with him early to Kingston to prepare for school in the fall.

He didn't want to be cheated out of more time at Stone Mills. With a haunted lake to explore, he wasn't ready for summer to end just yet.

Chapter 3

~~~

Milling About

Kingston's streets are wide and frightening. Stone taverns and brick storefronts in row after row of crooked lines are etched upon the landscape. Faceless people are moving about, mingling in dishevelled clothes or military uniforms. John can see the April sun is low in the sky, as it always is in this dream.

The edges of the dark tavern are blurry and threatening. How many times has John been here? He has the same dream almost every month. The shapes of the buildings change, shrinking and growing without reason. The faceless people rise and fall in number. But the end result is always the same. For six, long years, the dream has always been the same.

First, the alcohol. The foul taste of whisky pressed hard against his seven-year-old lips. Worse, he must watch as his younger brother, James, endures the same. The man's gruff hands grab the back of his little brother's head. He forces him closer to the bottle, even as John hangs from the man's arm, pleading that he stop. Two other men snort their approval from their corner of the tavern.

As the man momentarily walks to the bar to buy more alcohol, John does what he always does in this dream. He makes the same mistake over and over – the one that kills his little brother. He grabs his brother's hand and they run.

John bursts through the tavern door, the pounding sound of mindless laughter ringing in his ears behind him.

No, don't run this time!

As usual, the John that he sees running, with James barely keeping up, doesn't listen. The sound of the tavern door opening a second time with a terrible slam overwhelms his ears. He runs faster. They make it only to the large oak tree when little James stumbles, falling flat on his face and scraping his right cheek. It's then that the lumbering man, Kennedy, catches up to them and raises a thick, wooden cane. In his dream, John never sees the impact of the cane. He cries over top of his younger brother, vaguely aware of the fleeing, distorted shape of the man who once worked for his father's store in Kingston.

Nearly dawn. John awakens in sweat. Light offers itself through his tiny window as he pulls the blanket over his eyes. He has to be at the mill soon to start work. He has to forget the unforgettable.

***

"Sorry, George," said John, out of hearing range of the farmer they were helping. "I didn't know we'd be this busy."

George shrugged good-naturedly as he unloaded another bushel of wheat just outside of the stone mill. A year younger than John and French speaking, George Cloutier was never mistaken for John's brother, although they had fast become friends. John's free-flowing, dark curls, large nose and lean, tall frame was in contrast to George's stockier, shorter build with a thick head of straight, greased hair.

John tried to put last night's dream out of his mind, losing himself in the anticipation of exploring once the work was done.

"That is okay, mon ami – looks like we are almost done anyway." He tossed the last bushel of wheat to the men in the mill and then they paused to watch. They surveyed the mill's heavy stone, three feet wide, turn against a stationary stone with grooves cut into it from the centre to the ends. After the grain was ground, it eventually fell from the outer edges of the two stones.

The wheel's turns were powered from the waterfall cascading over Lake of the Mountain. Sifting the flour was done by hand above bins in the basement. Then the flour was hoisted up ladders to the second level where it was dumped on the floor to be raked back and forth until it cooled. After that, other men had to strain it by hand using a crank-powered flour sifter.

With all the dust flying around from the mill work, George instinctively felt to make sure his hair was intact. As usual, it was combed straight back and held in place with grease from his mother's cooking lard.

"I cannot believe you have to go back to Kingston soon," said George. "Soon I will have to watch out for Owen all by myself."

After telling George about his encounter with Owen yesterday, John wondered if his friend was more worried about his stiff hair being messed up than he was anything else. "Owen's an oaf," he said, looking over his shoulder. "You'll be fine."

John scrunched his shoulders down and hoarsely whispered, "Anyway, forget him. Maybe later we can explore...you know...where Whisky Wilson was."

He eyed the trees behind them and George looked up at the looming, forested mountain. "Sure – as long as we can stay away from the saw mill," said George. He lowered his voice further. "I am not going near that place."

John laughed. George's French accent always sounded more dramatic when he whispered.

"Come on, George, you've got to learn to have more fun. What could Mr. Pitman do, really?"

"He works with saw blades, John – do you not have an imagination?"

John kept working as he grinned. "I can't promise anything my friend. Sometimes it's fun to sneak a peek at Mr. Pitman – have you seen how much wood he can lift with his bare hands?"

Nathaniel Pitman, the saw mill owner, was a towering man and one of the most feared men in the village. He rarely had a word to say and seemed to have no friends in Stone Mills. On the other hand, he ran the only saw mill in the area which made him indispensable.

John wanted to explore Lake on the Mountain but he loved the waters of the Bay of Quinte, too, which were practically right outside their door. Long stretches of water cut Prince Edward County off from the mainland, making it feel like an island. Anyone travelling to the county for the first time was always amazed at the scenery. Quiet bays, rocky bluffs, finely-sketched shores and reaches of long, watery fingers for miles.

John saw his father happily talking to customers. That always put him in a great mood.

The perfect time to see if George and I can get out of here.

A movement caught John's eye. He looked diagonally

across the tiny village toward Pringle's General Store. Stone Mills was small enough that everyone could see what others were doing if they were outside and paying attention.

A baby-faced man with large eyes and a small nose and chin stepped out onto the porch, closely followed by the store's proprietor, Hannah Pringle. John recognized the man as Darius Marshall, a farmer from the top of the mountain. Darius and Hannah said something to one another and then the farmer hopped up onto his wagon. It became obvious he was directing his team of horses toward the Macdonald's mill.

"Is he coming here?" asked George.

John sighed. "I think so. Looks like a full load."

Chapter 4

Darius

John watched Hannah Pringle linger for a moment on her porch before returning inside. Darius Marshall couldn't stop smiling as he pulled his team up alongside the mill. That didn't necessarily mean he was happy. Many people who knew him said it was more of a facial tick than a smile. He just couldn't control it.

The horses made restful sounds as they were tied to a post. Darius, a middle-aged man with a younger man's stride, hopped to the ground. His smile was pasted firmly to his baby-shaped face.

"Howdy boys – well look at you two now. You look like someone just drank your last cup of tea, yes siree. That's what we Brits drink all the time, right?"

John and George exchanged glances. British people didn't often refer to themselves as Brits. John also realized he didn't seem to know George had a French background, not British.

"We're fine, Mr. Marshall, sir," said John. "We're

ready to work."

"I see, I see," he said, scratching his smooth chin while reading John's face. "You young fellows were about to leave this place and find something fun to do. And then I pull up and ruin everything. Tell you what, I'm not one to wreck anyone's good time so let's work together quickly on this. If anyone else tries to drop their grain off, well…I'll give them the evil eye, like this." He rolled his eyes around in his head and John and George laughed.

Darius Marshall had moved from York – which some folks still called Toronto – to Stone Mills about a year ago. But John didn't know why he had ever left York for such a rural life.

The round-faced farmer was strong and swift in his movements. He worked quickly with John and George and within twelve minutes the wheat had been stacked along the back wall in the mill.

"Thank ya kindly, boys," he said. He reached into his pocket and tossed an American five-cent piece to each of them.

"Wow, thank you Mr. Marshall," said John.

"Yes, thank you," echoed George.

John had long observed that Upper Canada was a medley of currencies. One never knew what to expect when it came time for payment. John had seen his father paid in American bank notes and coins, Bank of

Montreal dollar notes from Lower Canada or British pound notes from the Bank of Upper Canada. Even copper coins and tokens of differing quality were still accepted, despite discouragement from the banks. John knew his father would take them. The most common form of exchange was simply to barter.

Darius looked up and down the dusty path of a road. "Looks like you two are freer than songbirds," he announced. "That is, if you can convince your father."

John ran inside the mill again and found his father still talking to his customers. He easily got permission to spend time with George and they flew out of the mill. Darius, still smiling, tipped his hat to John and George as they ran by.

Their immediate destination had changed with money in their pockets. They swooped past Abraham Steel's tavern and over to Pringle's General Store.

"That was nice," panted George. "The way Monsieur Marshall helped us."

John nodded. "Let's hurry – I heard she was getting low on hard candy."

John bolted up the stairs of Pringle's General Store just as his mother was exiting.

"My word and what are you both doing here?" she said. She adjusted the basket in her hand and eyed John and George as if they were horse thieves.

"Mother!" said John in surprise. "Father said George

and I could go to the store – Mr. Marshall gave us both a five-cent piece." He held it in front of her as shining proof of legitimacy. George followed suit.

"Lord love a duck! It's still morning!" Helen said. "You think you need candy in the morning?"

John wondered why candy might taste different in the morning instead of the afternoon but he sensed it was one of those times to keep quiet.

Just a few more seconds.

"Well, go on with you both. Spend it fast in case it burns a hole in your trousers."

John knew the permission would come. It paid to learn how to read people and he had realized long ago that he was good at it.

"Bye Mother."

"Au revoir," Mrs. Macdonald."

"Yes, yes…" she muttered. John could still hear his mother talking to herself as they bolted up the stairs and into the store. John inhaled the scent of fresh spices as they opened the door and he breathed deeply, as if to save it for later. He couldn't imagine living on a farm, far from civilization. He liked the hustle and bustle of Kingston and even the small village charm of Stone Mills.

"Good Mornin' boys. Well if it isn't another Macdonald – and a Cloutier, too."

John and George looked up to see Hannah Pringle.

She was also known as the most eligible widow in all of Stone Mills and surrounding area, if adult gossip was to be believed. Her hair was long, straight and a faded gold, now streaked with grey.

The grey came over the months that followed Mr. Asa Pringle's death on Lake Ontario three years ago. A capsized boat had claimed the man's life, just before the Macdonald's had arrived in Stone Mills. Hannah found herself a widow at thirty-four and still one at thirty-seven. It wasn't from a lack of suitors interested in her but it might have had something to do with her perfectionist streak. That's what the adults said.

John let his eyes travel across the store, taking in the long, maple shelves bracketed to the wall, holding an assortment of coffee, tea, spices and cans of raisins. Hanging from the ceiling were dried meats, smoked and salted to help them last longer. His eyes glazed over the dry goods section, filled mainly with materials like bolts of cloth, thread, ribbon, needles and pins. This was Moll's favourite section, since she loved to sew. George pointed to the glass display case in front of the counter and John nodded. They knelt briefly to look at the knives.

"Now are you two just lookin' today or can I fetch you somethin' in particular?"

John beamed as he produced the five-cent piece and George followed suit. "Mr. Marshall gave us these," said John.

"For helping unload his wagon," said George.

"Now wasn't that nice," said Hannah, smiling longer than John expected. She walked past them to the front door and looked out towards the mill. John wondered what she was looking at and then saw Mr. Marshall glancing this way from the mill and smiling. Even though he always looked like he was grinning, John thought that this time it might be real somehow. He watched him tip his hat to her as she played with the ends of her hair.

"Uhh, Mrs. Pringle?" said John.

"Miss," she said quickly. Her smile ebbed and then returned softly as she twisted her bare, ring finger. She marched into the centre of the store and began sliding a heavy pickle barrel into a different position. Observing the minor change she moved behind the wooden counter. As she did, a few of *The Stone Mills Reformer* news sheets whooshed off onto the floor. John bent down and picked them up, re-reading the headlines he had already seen at home.

"Who do you think is printing these, Miss Pringle?" John asked. She took them from John and straightened them again, shaking her head.

"I really couldn't say," she said. "I just believe in givin' them some space. Healthier to have different opinions, I think."

George read some of the headlines. "'Responsible Government: It's Time.'" "What is responsible government, anyway?"

"It's government that's more accountable to people instead of what we have now," she said. "You must have heard the adults talk about the Family Compact?"

George and John nodded. "You mean the Tories, right?" John asked.

She nodded. "Some people are calling them that because it's a small number of families, controlled by men folk, who make sure they do whatever they want whenever they want." She lowered her voice. "Some people say they especially enjoy stuffin' their own pockets with money. Not that I'm saying that, you understand."

The boys nodded. "But we have an elected assembly," said John. "Right?"

"Yes, with no real say. If the Family Compact doesn't like a decision made by the Assembly, they just over-rule it. Does that sound right to you?"

John shook his head. "I guess not." He made a mental note to ask the colonel a few questions about Hannah's comments. She began stacking a new shipment of brown sugar on a thick wooden shelf. "Maybe the Americans know what they're doin down there after all. I mean, that's what some folks say."

***

Slurping on caramel hard candy and peppermint sticks, John and George moved behind the mill where the great, forested hill loomed. A few feet away they watched the thick thread of white, churning water shoot over the mountainside. From behind the waterfall, a pile of rocks stuck out on either side. Long ago, when loyalists first came upon the land, John had heard that the waterfall was like a white sheet.

A rustling noise in the woods gave John pause. He pointed to where he had seen the foliage moving a few feet away. George nodded and they took a step toward the sound. Just then a grizzled, grey-haired man popped his head out. John and George leapt back in surprise.

The man's face was weathered and worn and he licked at his lips which were lost behind a shock of grey beard. He blinked away the bright morning sun and focused on John and George. Sticking out his long, spindly arm he curled his index finger in a movement that could only mean 'follow me.' Then he disappeared back into the woods.

"Who…" George began.

John leaned in. "Could that be Jeremiah Thacker?"

"If it is, my father says he is crazy," said George. He tapped his head at the temple.

"Hi John!"

Oh no...here comes Lou.

"Hello, George. What are you doing?" She patted George's larded-down hair. "Good work on your hair today, George. Say, are you both going into the woods?"

George felt for damage to his stiff hair, while John clamped his hand over his sister's mouth. "Shh. Don't be so loud. Yes, we're going into the woods."

She pried his fingers from her mouth. "I want to come, too!"

Lou loved dangerous situations as much as he did, John knew. He stared anxiously into the thick trees. "Okay, but keep your mouth closed, you understand? I mean it, Lou."

She nodded, smiling. Underneath a thick canopy of oak and maple trees, John, George and Lou plunged into the forest behind the stone flour mill in pursuit of the strange man.

Chapter 5

Treasure

John caught sight of the old man again in the distance, walking straight up the side of the two-hundred-foot mountain. They trudged after him through the brush, looking for some semblance of a pathway.

"I think he's going all the way up to the lake," said John, digging his heels into the mix of leaves, soil and twigs. John's feet were bare, as were George and Lou's. No one wanted their shoes ruined from playing outside when they were so expensive to replace.

"Remind me again why we are following a crazy man into the forest?" George asked. He swiped bugs away as he walked. The hill was a dramatic, steep incline from this angle. Most adults went around the mountain where a rough road gradually led to the top. Going straight up the mountain from the bay side was only for the young and the young-at-heart.

"Keep your voice down...you said he was crazy, I didn't," corrected John. "I said most people think that."

John grabbed the rough bark of a massive, maple tree for support as he stooped to climb the great hill. The mountainous ridge of thick forest had already swallowed them whole. They were invisible to anyone near the mill or along the shore of the bay. The sound of the waterfall cascading over the side of the mountain behind the mill created a constant, tranquil background noise.

John caught sight of the wiry, old man again who had obviously made it to the top. He was standing upright until he was confident that John had seen him and then disappeared over the ridge.

"We're almost there," said John. "Come on."

"But what if he goes right to the edge of the lake?" asked George. Lou looked up with wide eyes. John recognized the anxiousness in George's voice and the apprehension in his sister's eyes.

"The lake is not haunted. There's no such thing – hurry up!"

John, George and Lou made it to the edge and grabbed hold of smaller saplings to finish pulling themselves to the edge of the great hilltop. They ran a few feet and then looked back. The webs and fingers of waterways known as the Bay of Quinte extended for miles around. It was a view John never tired of seeing.

Yet only thirty-feet away was an even greater marvel. Following the narrow waterfall which ran over the cliff, the three arrived at the edge of a small, impossible lake which provided the water's source. The locals called it Van Alstine's lake, after the Van Alstine family who were the first settlers of the area. But John and George preferred to call it Lake on the Mountain.

The lake shared its water freely, sending it over the cliff to power Hugh Macdonald's flour mill at the bottom. But what made the lake nearly impossible was that it had no known water source. How the lake continued to remain at the same level was the subject of much speculation. Many people believed there was an underground spring which fed it all the way from Lake Erie. Then there was the Mohawk's theory. They called it Onokenoga, or Lake of the Gods, and believed that spirits dwelled within its deep waters. Each spring the Mohawk offered gifts to the spirits to ensure a successful crop in the coming year.

"Let's go!" John said, running for the lake, deftly side-stepping the trees. The forest was thinner here where settlers had cleared them for their nearby homes and farmland. As the tallest and fastest, John arrived first and came to an abrupt stop as he reached Lake on the Mountain. No matter how many times he encountered the calm waters, it always took his breath away. Even though the mountain was more like a very large hill or mountainous ridge, the fact that a lake could be sitting on top was nonetheless extraordinary.

"I don't see him, John," said George. "Did we lose him?"

"Here," said a wobbly voice from behind them. A man emerged from behind a maple tree, more twisted and weathered than the tree that had hidden him. His sand-coloured pants were ripped and dirty at the knees. A long-sleeved, plaid shirt was open, revealing great curls of grey chest hair.

"The name's Jeremiah Thacker...and I want to give you something."

Everyone froze. "Sit, now. Sit," he said, extending his hand to a fallen birch tree. "Old Jeremiah's not goin' to hurt you."

The three looked behind them at the fallen birch and sat slowly, saying nothing.

"I was only fourteen – not much older than you two," the man said. He sat on a rotted tree stump two feet away and faced them, his eyes hungry and tired.

"Guess it was 1759. Yes – that's the year. I was walkin' along the shore 'bout a mile from here – just walkin,' lookin for tall ships. Didn't know what my life held. You see, my father died young. When that happened, my Ma – well, she took off and made a life somewhere. Don't know where – but it wasn't with me, that much I can tell you."

John started to take a breath as if he were about to speak but Jeremiah held up a withered hand.

"So I was tryin' to figure out what to do with my life. That's when I found him, just crawlin' along the shore, leavin' a trail of blood."

"Who?" blurted George.

"A sailor," Jeremiah answered. "Not just any sailor – a French admiral. Back then, the Seven Years War was on, you have to remember. Battles were all down the big lakes and in the port towns. The British were mounting forces in the area for some of the final battles of the war. So I ran up to him and I made him look at me – so I could see his eyes. Even then, I knew he was a goner."

The old man pointed to his own eyes to explain. "It was as if there weren't enough life left in the eyes. That admiral, he was tryin' to say somethin' to me, before he died."

"What did he…" John began.

"What did he say?" Lou blurted at the same time.

"Take this," Jeremiah said softly.

John looked puzzled. The old man grabbed John by the wrist and pretended to force something into his hand. Jeremiah's eyes were ablaze.

"He said, 'take this.' That's all he said. And that's when he died – and my life ended." He let go of John's wrist. John rubbed it instinctively but didn't take his eyes off Jeremiah.

"What was it?" asked John.

"What was it? Thought it was everythin,' that's what. Thought it was the answer for my life," said the old man. He scratched one side of his wild, grey hair and caused some of it to stick out.

"Didn't know it would be the only thing I'd ever come to know."

"He gave you a map," John said. He took a chance that the rumours he had heard about the old man were true. "It was a treasure map."

Jeremiah stood from the stump he was sitting on and cackled. "Map, maybe. Treasure map? My whole life says it can't be. Can't be."

He stood in silence for a moment and John, George and even Lou tried to stay quiet, too.

"But what if it is real?" Jeremiah finally said. "Spent my whole life believin.' Maybe it just wasn't for me to find. Maybe it will be for someone else."

Jeremiah reached into a roughly-sewn inside pocket of his patched shirt. He pulled out a curled scroll of paper, battered and frayed. "Here – take it." The older man thrust the map into John's startled hand.

"Don't know if it's real," the man said as John unfurled the map with George and Lou crowded around each of his shoulders. It was roughly drawn, with arrows pointing behind – or into – what looked like lines representing the trees of a forest. It looked like he may have tried to draw a large hill, but the lines could also have been something else, John reasoned.

"Always thought the treasure was on this mountain somewhere here in the forest, near 'bout where I found the admiral. When I couldn't find anythin' I began to explore the entire area between here and Kingston by foot, back and forth, lookin' for an area that seemed similar. Even went west, past Hallowell, to where the shores are nothing but sand for as far as the eye can see."

John had heard of the great sand shores west of Hall-owell but had never seen them.

"I'm no closer for it," the old man added. "Maybe it is here but not meant for one like me."

"Why give it to us?" asked John.

The old man shrugged. "I've seen you around, here and there. You seem to have lots of family, unlike me. Hopefully that'll make all the difference. Give you perspective, maybe. Never had anyone do that for me – never had anyone to help shape me."

"Did any friends help you search?" asked George.

He shook his head. "Likely a mistake. I didn't want any friends. You see, gold and money does that to a person – sometimes even just the thought of it. Leaves you mistrustful. Makes you do crazy things. I was afraid of what would happen if I let go of this 'til it became all I knew."

"Where will you go?" asked John. "What with no

family and all."

The man tried to chuckle and re-scratched his head, somehow fixing the tuft of hair that had been sticking out. "No family, true. Too late for that. But I'm going to try to let this go. Maybe explore some new place without thinking of maps or gold. Maybe I'll head northwest – see what's beyond Upper Canada."

"Beyond Upper Canada?" said George. "There's nothing there."

"That's what folks always say 'til they find something," said Jeremiah. He wished them well then turned on his heel and abruptly moved deeper into the forest before they could properly thank him.

After Jeremiah left, John huddled around George and Lou. John said, "Don't you remember hearing any stories about the man who has spent his whole life looking for treasure, somewhere between Kingston and Stone Mills?"

"Yes, but I didn't think it was true," said George, eyes wide.

"No one can know about this. Not Mother, not Father, not Colonel Macpherson – no one."

Lou frowned. "What about Moll?"

Another sound made all three friends swing their heads around. John shrugged as a large black bird moved from one tree to another. John let his eye travel the perimeter of the lake.

"Okay, you're right. No one except Moll. But that's it," said John firmly.

"I want to help search, John," said Lou.

John sighed. "You can help look sometimes. But I'm not guaranteeing you can always come. You're not old enough to always play with George and me."

Lou made a scoffing sound and cracked a twig with her bare heel in frustration. John ignored her and looked around. Then his face brightened.

"Before we look for treasure we should peek into the saw mill since we're already here. Maybe we'll get to see Mr. Pitman yelling at his employees."

George shook his head. "Let us just stay here…"

But John was already moving.

"John!" called out George in a hushed tone.

"Come on George," said Lou. "I'll protect you."

"That is not funny," he said, scrambling behind Lou.

The great, wood-framed building rose up on the edge of the mountain, dark and hungry. He peeked through a missing chunk of wood in one of the building's planks to see the monster within. There, hunched over a long plank of wood with one of his employees, was Nathaniel Pitman. Lou bumped him on the arm and whispered, "Let me see."

Although it was true that they usually stayed away from the saw mill, John couldn't always resist. It felt exhilarating to be peering through its walls. The mill was the opposite of his father's flour mill, John realized. The Macdonald mill was a community hub where people came to gossip and share information; this mill was lonely and silent, other than the sounds of sawing and cutting.

The three of them took turns watching from their vantage point at a corner of the mill. John watched the huge saw, held taut on its upward stroke by a spring pole overhead. Nathaniel Pitman and another man, slim and muscular, worked the saw up and down using a wooden beam attached to a crank on the mill wheel.

A few moments later it was George's turn to watch but he declined. "No, thank you – Lou can have my turn, too," he said, whispering hoarsely.

"Oh, you really do like me – thank you, George," she said, patting his thickly-larded hair. George winced. John could see Lou looking perplexed as she stared through the crevice of the board.

"What's wrong, Lou?"

"I don't see Mr. Pitman."

John and George looked at one another, confused. Then everyone lost the warmth of the sun. Finding themselves in a great shadow, John, George and Lou turned around. Standing over them was a great, bearded eclipse.

Nathaniel Pitman.

Lou screamed. John clamped a hand over her mouth.

"What are you doing here?" demanded the towering man. His eyes were small and dark, lost in his deep-set brow. His voice was deep and rumbling and infringed on the solitude of the lake.

"We…" began George.

"We were fishing at the lake," completed John, smiling through his nervousness.

"We were?" blurted Lou, who suddenly found herself with her brother's hand over her mouth again.

The giant of a man looked around. "Where are your poles?"

"Poles?" repeated George, as if it was the most ridiculous, follow-up question imaginable.

"Oh, we don't use poles, sir," said John. "We're just using our hands – like bears do." John mimicked the action of a swatting bear in a stream and then glanced toward George who also began swatting in a make-believe river.

"You're very close to my saw mill. I don't like children near my mill," said the towering man, inching closer while stroking his long, dark beard.

"Yes, we were just talking about that and…oh, do you hear that?" John cocked his head to one side with exaggeration.

The heavy-breathing saw mill operator frowned and stopped. "Hear what?"

"It's my mother," John and George both blurted out

at once. John glared at George.

"It's his mother," they both pointed at one another. In the corner of his eye John saw Lou bolt for the edge of the mountain. John grabbed George by the shoulder and ran after her.

Chapter 6

The Games People Play

The chess game mirrored John's mood. His queen was somehow trapped, his two knights were floundering, his bishops and one rook had long ago been taken and his pawns were nearly spent. It was not his finest game. Moll glanced up at her brother and didn't say anything, but John knew she was wondering how quickly to finish him off.

"What's bothering you?" she asked. They were playing chess in their customary seats in the main living area. A soft stream of morning light sliced across the wooden game board. Today, Lieutenant Colonel Donald Macpherson would arrive. Knowing he was coming reminded John of Kingston, which in turn had reminded him of his recent nightmare.

"Something's wrong. Is it the treasure map?" Moll asked. She looked toward the front door. However, Helen and Lou had not yet returned from the general store. John continued to sit with his head in his hands.

"No – it's not that. But thanks for sewing that inside pocket," said John, instinctively feeling the slight bulge in his vest where the map rested.

"You're welcome." Moll didn't press any further. Instead, she calmly killed another pawn with a swoop of her dark bishop.

"Moll, do you ever think of James – I mean, still?" He glanced into her sky blue eyes and saw her flinch.

"Of course I do."

John nodded. Reaching over he moved one of his knights in retreat. "Once in a while – quite often, really – I have the same terrible dream. I can see us in that tavern…James and me. With Kennedy." His eyes stared at the chess board.

"Kennedy's gone now," said Moll.

John raised his head. "So is James."

"I know that."

John sacrificed a pawn to her waiting queen. "What I mean is," said John, "I should have done more. That's why I think I keep dreaming it over and over again."

"John, you were young yourself, only a year-and-a-half older. You mustn't ever think that."

"I was still the eldest brother."

"You were seven-years-old John!" She looked at him with caring eyes. "Do you know why you keep dreaming about it?"

John felt his eyes begin to well as he shook his head.

"Because you were there!" she said. "You were the only one, out of all of us, who can carry James inside of you that way. You couldn't have done more than you did."

Using his shirt sleeve John absorbed a stray tear that had gotten through his resolve. "I won't forget him, Moll. Mother and Father may. But I won't."

Her eyes moist, she reached over to give him a hug.

"I'm still going to wallop you in this game you know."

"I know," said John, grinning.

***

It was the pain in his head that he felt first. It was as if a great boulder was resting on top of it.

Anson Rightmyer awoke, sitting. He was on a slim, splintered chair in a mud-dark cabin. He couldn't swallow. Not the way he wanted. A piece of dark, green cloth was tied tightly across his mouth and around his head. As he tried to move, Anson felt like he was a part of the chair. In a way, he realized he was. His arms were tightly bound behind him. In turn, his ankles were tied to the chair legs.

The last thing he remembered was seeing a shape in the lake. An impossible shape. Had he been attacked by…that thing? No. He had seen something…but it was from behind that he had been grabbed. He remembered the strong hand over his mouth.

Anson's eyes began to adjust to the pain in his head to see beyond the chair on which he sat. He squinted and saw three shapes. Two men were standing in front of him, a third figure on a chair, further back. The two men who were standing were impassive, stiff and soldier-like.

The man on the chair, though, was different. He was round-faced and stared back at him. Smiling. It wasn't a warm smile, though. Not at all. In fact it didn't seem like a smile at all – more like a twitch around the mouth. The grinning man gently stroked the back of a tiny, brown sparrow with his index finger.

Anson blinked. He knew this man – it was his neighbour! He had been found and would soon be going home! The rag in his mouth wouldn't allow him to work his tongue properly. But he moaned at the smiling man and tried to call his name.

"...ar-i-uhh...ar-i-uhh....!"

"Shhh," the voice came back. "It's too late for talking, too late. You're just too curious of a Brit you are. Just too curious."

Darius Marshall rose. He set the sparrow on a small table and swaddled it in cloth. On his belt Darius wore a long knife. He slowly drew it from its sheath and then selected an apple from a bin in the corner of the room.

Then he moved within inches of Anson's face.

Anson drained of all colour. Going home was far from certain, he realized. Something was wrong. Darius palmed the apple for a moment and then began to peel it directly in front of Anson's eyes. Each puncture of the apple's skin caused Anson's heart to tighten.

"I'm sorry. Is this bothering you?" asked Darius, nodding to the knife and apple. Anson nodded, unsure. The twitching face of his neighbour laughed. Then Darius raised the knife to the bridge of Anson's nose. Anson felt the cold touch of the knife's blade trace along the bridge of his nose and down its slope. The last thing he thought of was Mary Ann, just moments before he fainted.

Chapter 7

The Colour of Oppression

"Mother, when will the colonel be here?" asked John, bursting into the house for the second time. The smell of baking bread wafted through the room and John immediately felt like he could eat a second breakfast.

"Any moment," she said, sweeping the kitchen for the third time. Moll and Lou were polishing silverware and smirked at John. "If you'd just stay down by the bay instead of poking your head in here every five minutes, you just might be there to greet him."

"Is Colonel Macpherson travelling with Cornelius?" asked John.

"Yes, but don't you talk his poor ear off. And if being there to greet him doesn't sound like something you'd like to do, you can head back to the mill."

"No, no – I should be there to say hello! Bye now!" John fled from the house. Although it would be nice to see the colonel again, it would be even better to have time to hang out with George. But he wouldn't be available until this afternoon to explore, since the Cloutier's had family visiting.

John could hardly stand it, considering the map in his inside pocket. He had been up late, staring at the strange markings on it in the fading light of his room until his eyes bulged.

Although he boarded in a rooming house while he attended grammar school during the long, winter months in Kingston, the Macpherson's house was a second home to John. His uncle and Aunt Anna were always there for him.

John often felt like he lived two completely different lives. One was full of the kind of excitement that can only be found in a larger city. On Kingston's busy streets all manner of people could be found. On a Friday night John could go about the town and watch men and women from high society move about the city in their expensive clothes. Yet all around them were the desperate poor, and homeless, living like animals between taverns and shops.

Recent immigrants from England, Scotland and Ireland – as the Macdonald's had once been – mixed with officers and soldiers from Kingston's great military presence. It was a diverse blend of people, trying to live their lives in many different ways.

John remembered some of the trip across the Atlantic Ocean in the ship, 'Earl of Buckinghamshire,' when he was just five years old. It wasn't an easy voyage, being stuck in the cargo hold area with other poor immigrants looking for a new life in a new land.

His other life, here in Stone Mills, was another world. This summer was even more remarkable than usual, given that he had a treasure map in his pocket and rumours of a lake creature in his head – all in the same summer. John's only wish was that he had more time.

As he looked across the water, John couldn't see anything other than the ferryman, Jacob Adams, taking someone across the reach to Adolphustown. The ferry service – which was a flat-bottom boat called a bateau – constantly made the brief trip back and forth, like an aquatic road for travellers.

Adolphustown was less than a mile away on the other side by ferry and was one of the first settlements in Prince Edward County. It was where John had previously attended school.

A couple of years ago, the Macdonald's had lived in Hay Bay, which was also across the water's reach. Back then, John walked to school from Hay Bay to Adolphustown every morning and night, a distance of three miles, one way. The small, wooden schoolhouse where he attended had been built by the original settlers, the United Empire Loyalists, who had fled the American Revolution. They sacrificed everything in order to remain part of Great Britain.

John watched the ferryman and now two other men fishing at the edge of the bay. He still didn't see anything else. This area of Upper Canada had so many inlets it was difficult to see in a straight line. One moment, a person could see a vessel and then the next, it would be gone as it steered around a sharp corner of the bay.

While he waited, John walked down the shoreline to Solomon Brook's shipbuilding and repair business. He could see Solomon shaping a piece of oak as he drew closer. John eyed the half-of-a-ship being built while resting on large blocks along the sandy shore. He wondered where this new vessel might be headed. Perhaps Kingston, Montreal or even overseas to England?

The burly, red-headed man nodded to John as he approached. There probably wasn't a larger, stronger man in Stone Mills, except for maybe Nathaniel Pitman.

"John, lad – how are you faring this morning?" asked Solomon. He leaned the great plank of oak he was working on against the fledgling ship.

"I'm well, thank you, Mr. Brook."

"Waiting for your uncle, I presume?"

"How did you know?"

Solomon used his forearm to wipe his face. "It's not hard to figure out what goes on in a village this size, lad" he laughed. "The colonel's a good man. I've met him a couple of times."

"He's coming with Cornelius," John said. "Maybe he had a delayed load."

Solomon scoffed. "Cornelius Larue has always been delayed. I can't understand why your uncle would travel with that character – a man of his stature deserves better."

John grinned. "The colonel likes to help people out – he likely wanted to give Cornelius the extra work."

"Sure," said Solomon, "as long as the poor colonel doesn't have to pay with his life. He's a braver man than me."

Cornelius' bateau was a thirty-footer, pointed at both ends. It was larger than the local ferryman's, but was on the older side. For years Solomon had been trying to sell Cornelius a new one.

The boat was a common sight between Stone Mills and Kingston, as he made his living moving goods from place to place in what was becoming a busy trade area. Bateau operators like Cornelius made it possible for businesses like the Macdonald's mill to find a market for its flour. Hugh Macdonald sold most of his flour into the larger Kingston and Montreal markets. And it was also how finished goods like sugar, spices and cloth came to tiny Stone Mills.

Even though there was a rough road called the 'Danforth' which crept along Lake Ontario between Kingston and Ancaster, people still preferred travel by water given the torturous quality of the road. The waterways, lakes, rivers and inlets provided reliable four-season roads and became pathways for people and goods in everything from canoes, skiffs, scows and bateaux.

"Did you hear about Anson Rightmyer?" asked Solomon.

John shook his head. He knew of Mr. Rightmyer, a farmer on top of Lake on the Mountain. Whenever John saw him at the mill he couldn't help but stare at the man's four-fingered hand, even though he knew it was rude.

"Looks like he disappeared. He was supposed to help the Goslin's with their crop, since they were taking turns helping each other out – you know how it works," he said.

John nodded. Farming wasn't an easy life and neighbours always helped each other at harvest time.

"He better not have skipped town, that's all I can say," said Solomon.

"Why would he do that?"

"Well, I shouldn't be spreading this around, but the man owed me a crop share for some work I helped him with. I'm still waiting for it, and now he's disappeared. Hmmph," added Solomon.

"It hasn't been too long, though, right?" asked John. "Maybe he went hunting?"

"Yeah, likely he got lost somewhere while hunting, more like it. That man hasn't been right in the head since Mary Ann died anyway."

John didn't know what to think about Mr. Rightmyer's state of mind. He barely knew the man.

"Well, look along there, lad. That's them now," said Solomon, scratching his red beard and nodding at the bay. "I'm surprised they're still afloat."

John followed Solomon's gaze out onto the bay. Having rounded an inlet, the bateau was now visible. Cornelius, lanky, with blonde, dishevelled hair, was only partly visible to John's line of sight. That's because his uncle was standing on the bow of the small bateau as if his were the lead ship in a great armada in some grand military manoeuvre. John waved and danced around.

***

He moved unseen and unheard. Among the thick shrubs and long grass, Darius Marshall watched the open water of the Bay of Quinte from his elevated hiding place.

As he scrutinized the great bay, he stole glances toward the general store. Darius couldn't help but picture Hannah Pringle. She was so different from Sophia, and he thanked his lucky stars for that. Hannah would never run off with another man. His face darkened.

Least of all a member of the Family Compact.

Darius squinted. He could see a bateau approaching on the open water. Normally this was not surprising. Stone Mills had its fair share of visitors and traders. But this time, the approaching vessel concerned him. He took cover to watch until the bateau grew closer. His keen eyes spotted a smudge of red in the flat-bottomed boat. British red. The colour of oppression. The colour he had voluntarily fought against as a member of the U.S. army, earning his reputation under Colonel Richard Johnson as a mounted rifleman. He remembered the clash of bayonets along the Thames River, east of Detroit, against the 41st Regiment of Foot.

The Brits had surrendered there with their Indian allies as they would in the near future once his own plan was complete. The biggest mistake his country had ever made was signing the Treaty of Ghent to end the War of 1812. They had given up too soon. They had not committed to the war the way he had personally committed to it.

He was grateful to have the support of some of the top men from his old unit here in the village. They trusted him completely – even his eccentric approaches to battle.

The bateau drew nearer and he began to recognize the small vessel and its operator, Cornelius Larue. But the red uniform moved to the front of the bateau and perched there, like a bloated hawk. Yes, he was a Brit all right. An officer of some kind. But he looked old. Washed up. Probably should be retired if he's not already. Odd – but not a threat.

A movement caught his eye. He could see the burly red-headed shipbuilder. But it was the young Macdonald boy on shore who was moving, jumping up and down and waving warmly to the Brit as if he knew him well. Perhaps he was even a relative.

Too bad. He knew the Macdonald's were Brits but he didn't know their connection to the British military. That wouldn't do. That wouldn't do at all. He would have to consider them all hostile now. People like the Macdonald's didn't know what democracy looked like. Living like this, under foreign rule, they were a malignant presence.

He wondered what President Adams would say once he handed him Stone Mills, the perfect point from which to lead troops to Kingston and York. He wondered if Hannah would marry him for the great man that he was about to become.

Chapter 8

Macpherson

As the bateau drew closer, Lieutenant Colonel Donald Macpherson's posture heightened. He was wearing his full British military uniform, his own eccentricity considering he was a retired officer. John remembered his father saying the colonel was the kind of person who could never really retire. He saluted John in mock greeting while standing on the bow. John smartly saluted back the way his uncle had taught him years ago.

Cornelius Larue didn't operate the largest bateau in the Bay of Quinte-Kingston area but he rarely had an empty one, either. It was partly thanks to his reasonable rates but also because of his personality. He had the kind of intelligence that worked well in dealing with people, even though he had little formal schooling. Cornelius plied his trade along Lake Ontario and its many bays, carrying goods back and forth between Kingston and the small communities to the west.

The bateau – which he had dubbed *Morning Bloom* –

shifted abruptly and the officer lost his stance. Cornelius, slope-shouldered and wiry, gripped the long pole used in the operation of the bateau and suppressed a smile.

"Can you handle this no-good, floating death trap?" asked the colonel. He was red-faced at having lost his regal stance.

"My apologies, Colonel," said Cornelius. He hopped out of the boat onto the shore. The boatman dragged one foot behind him, leaving single footprints and a streak of sand. Despite his pronounced limp, he could move quickly.

"Do you need any help, Mr. Larue?" asked John.

"No, no thank you, John." As he moved to tie up his boat he caught John looking at his leg.

"This old thing? Not too graceful on land, is it?" he said, patting his leg. It's probably why I prefer the open water, where a man's legs don't matter much."

John smiled. The colonel grumbled as he warily climbed out.

"That's better – land. Not so many variables now."

John approached the colonel and shook his uncle's hand. "It's good to see you sir," said John. "How is everything in Kingston?"

"All the duller without your company, but otherwise just fine my boy." John laughed. As he studied the colonel's face he decided his father was probably right.

This was no ordinary visit.

Solomon Brook approached, wiping off wood shavings from his shirt. John noticed that he carried a paper in one hand. He shook the colonel's hand and exchanged pleasantries. John surmised that working along the bay ensured Solomon got to know most everyone who arrived by water. The shipbuilder handed the colonel the paper, then wandered over to Cornelius' bateau and knocked on the wood. "Cornelius – I see you're still using this tiny death-trap with its leaky planks."

"It's not tiny, it's manoeuvrable," said Cornelius, patting the boat like a child while he secured it. "And she has a name, you know – it's *Morning Bloom*. Or you may simply call her *The Bloom* if you'd like."

"The shipbuilder in me thinks of her more as *The Doom*," said Solomon.

Cornelius sighed while John smothered a smirk. "I'm surprised you sell any ships with your personality," said the bateau operator.

"I'm surprised you're not my best customer," said Solomon. "My men can build you something that will last a lifetime, if you should change your mind."

"I'll keep that in mind," said Cornelius, "although she shows no signs of fatigue." He banged on the boat to demonstrate and a splinter of wood flew off and stuck to Solomon's shirt.

"Here," said Solomon, handing it back to him. "You might need this to get back home." Cornelius mumbled something under his breath. Solomon turned his attention toward the British officer, who was absorbed in the news sheet. "The latest one just appeared a couple of days ago."

John realized the shipbuilder had handed the colonel a copy of *The Stone Mills Reformer,* the news sheet his father had been talking about earlier. Colonel Macpherson shook his head as he read the headlines.

"John, my boy, you better let me get settled in," said the colonel. "I've got work to do."

Chapter 9

The Lake Serpent

Deep into the forest John, George and Lou wandered, as brooding elms extended their arms to slow their progress. Pulling branches aside, John stopped and listened. Only the deceiving sounds of crickets filled the evening air and he paid them little heed.

"Well, do you see anything?" John asked.

George looked around. "Yes, oui my friend."

"What?"

"Trees – lots of trees," said George. He tried to suppress a smile and John slugged him in the arm.

"Ow!"

"Don't hit George," said Lou. She tried to pat his head but George shrunk away.

John squatted and unrolled the treasure map again. The colonel was now settled in and John had gone back to the mill to help his father for the rest of the afternoon. But he was now free and supper with the colonel wouldn't be until later in the evening. John regretted that Lou had to be included. Little sisters were so intrusive.

"Let's look again. I thought that perhaps this large tree stump here is near the treasure," said John.

George scowled. "You think that is a tree stump? I thought it was the stone pile where we made that hideout up by the lake," he said, squinting at the sketches on the map.

John sighed. "No wonder Mr. Thacker had so much trouble." He stood suddenly. "Let's head for the stone pile, then. We're halfway there anyway."

A few minutes later, out of breath from their climb, the three sat at the edge of Lake on the Mountain. The large pile of stones sat in silence on the north side of the lake. Settlers had stacked the rocks when they had cleared their fields years ago. From where they sat, they could see fields on either side and Nathaniel Pitman's saw mill on their left, to the south. But as John looked at the mound of stones there was no obvious place on top of the mountain where someone would have left treasure.

"I just realized there's one problem with your stone-pile theory," said John. "The French admiral who drew this map did it in...what...1759, according to Mr. Thacker. That's sixty-nine years ago! Probably a lot on the mountain has changed."

George looked at him and then it hit him too. "These

stones weren't here sixty-nine years ago!"

"Exactly," said John. "Or at least they weren't all in one pile like this – they were all over the fields before the farmers cleared them."

They looked out onto the quiet lake, where deep shadows were already thrown across its edges as the sun dropped further in the sky.

"Do you think we'll see what Whisky Wilson saw, John?" asked Lou.

John shrugged. "I'd love for the Mohawk legends to be true."

"Well, Monsieur Wilson said he saw a strange shape in the lake," said George.

"Whisky Wilson," said John.

"That's rude," said Lou.

"It's true," said John.

"Still rude."

"Still true."

George sighed. John shrugged and leaned in to speak more quietly. "All I'm saying is that you can't put much faith in what a drinker says."

John selected a small, smooth stone and executed a four-bounce skip across the lake.

"Why do you think your uncle is here?" George asked, switching topics.

"Partly that news sheet," said John. "I think they're worried that those kinds of attitudes about the government will reach Kingston."

Squatting low for his next throw, John miscalculated and plunged it into the evening water on first contact. "Also," John added, "I know the colonel is upset Father ever left Kingston. They always argue about that."

"Why would he care?" asked George, raising a bushy eyebrow.

"He hasn't exactly made it a secret that he believes Father made a mistake leaving Kingston years ago," said John. "He thinks he should have made a better go of it in 'civilization' as he calls it. And never mind repeating any of this, Lou, or I won't bring you up here anymore."

Lou stuck her tongue out at John and then quickly retreated when John glared at her. She smiled sweetly at George who ignored her and fingered a smooth stone he found. "My parents sometimes miss Montreal," he conceded. "Running a farm is a lot…different here," said George, searching for the right word in English.

John didn't say anything but he wondered how difficult it could be when the Cloutier's had several farm workers to help them out. They were country squires from Montreal, looking to have a quieter lifestyle in the Stone Mills area.

John instinctively felt his inside vest pocket now and then to make sure the bulge of map was still there. Looking over at the looming saw mill, he turned to

George. "Let's go around to the other side of the lake. This is where we were before when Mr. Pitman came up beside us."

George whirled around. "Not the tree!" George said.

"Yes, of course the tree," said John.

Lou smiled at George. "I'll look after you, George."

"Stop saying that! Now why must we go to the tree?" George asked.

There was one tree on the lake that was an obvious favourite for young people who liked a bit of risk and danger. John knew George Cloutier was not one of those young people, but he would drag him there nonetheless.

"Come on, George – you don't have to actually be on the tree. Follow me."

A twisted oak, magnificent in size, arced over the water at an impossible angle. It was so bent and half uprooted that it allowed someone to climb far out onto the lake with an impressive number of tributary branches, too. As they walked along, John realized he wasn't seeing anything specific related to the map, as far as he could tell. He stopped abruptly.

"Do you hear something?"

"No – what is it?" asked Lou.

"I don't know." He looked behind them. "I thought I heard footsteps."

John shrugged and they kept going. Sullen oak and

maple trees competed with one another for space in a wide circle around the mysterious lake. Twilight had just begun to purple the lake and forest around it, creating an eerie sheen. Even though the days were longer now, the area around Lake on the Mountain was heavily treed and sheltered which muted the light. Now and then a clearing appeared where a farmer had painstakingly sawed trees and dug enough stumps to create lake access.

Arriving at the great oak, John balanced his way out over the lake beginning with its misshapen trunk. Lou followed closely behind while George stood at the base of the tree and folded his arms across his chest.

"Come on, George," said John without turning around. He knew his friend was waiting to be convinced. "Just a little ways out – the view is much better."

George kicked at a stone and watched it plunk in the water. "Fine. But not for long, right?"

"Of course not," said John.

They could see deep shadows further out, where the sprawling branches created a natural canopy over the water. George was nearly as far out as John and Lou.

"Be careful, John – you nearly slipped," said George. "If you drown you will just ruin the whole summer – do you not you remember the terrible drowning?"

John rolled his eyes. "No – and neither do you, George. It was before our time."

The tragedy happened where the Macdonald's had formerly lived, near Adolphustown across the water's reach. On August 29, 1819, ten years ago, eighteen people – most of them youth – had set out in a boat to attend church at the old Adolphustown Methodist Church. They had to cross Hay Bay from the west, about a mile-and-a-half wide on a clear morning.

When the boat started leaking, many people panicked which caused the boat to capsize. Only those people who could swim well or had the sense enough to hold onto the edge of the boat survived. Ten of the eighteen drowned. It was a local tragedy that everyone knew. Parents used it to warn their children to be careful near the water – like choosing not to walk on a bent tree hanging over a deep lake, for instance.

"Let's all sing the song," said Lou.

"No – not that dreadful song!" said George.

Most houses in the district still had copies of a song one of the pastors had written to remember the tragic day. Ignoring George, Lou picked out a verse.

"The boat being leaky, the water came in
To bale with their hats, they too late did begin.
They looked at each other and began for to weep.
The boat filled with water and sank in the deep."

"Hush up now, Lou," said John. He slowed and then

came to a stop. Lou swayed but righted herself before crashing into John. George barely stopped in time before hitting Lou.

"What's going on?" asked George.

"Why did you stop?" asked Lou.

John squinted in the shadows where the long tree branches hung in the water, a natural haven for fish and fishermen. "I thought I saw something in the lake."

George peered around their shoulders. "You are just kidding me, right? If you are joking, tell me now."

John resumed his careful movement along the bent oak. "Are you still worried about lake monsters?" asked John. "I told you it's Whisky Wilson's drinking and... Lou – stop shaking the tree!"

"It's not me!"

Raucous, familiar laughter prompted John to look back near the base of the tree.

Owen Boggart.

The hefty boy was shoving the tree as hard as he could at its base, making it difficult for the three to keep their balance. Not getting the result he was after, Owen edged his way closer up the length of the tree and began stomping with his full weight.

"Three of you at once – too good to be true," said Owen. He snickered and wheezed at the same time. It was all John, George and Lou could do to hang on.

As Owen looked up again to see if he was getting

close to toppling them, John noticed the boy's pie-shaped face had quickly drained of all colour. Owen hastily turned around, jumped from the tree, and fled. It was this last action – his weight leaving the tree so suddenly – that caused George to tumble over the side. John reached over Lou to try and grab him and then fell off the tree himself. Lou crouched down and hung on, avoiding them both.

Crying out the two boys hit the surface of the water at the same time. John surfaced first, sputtering and grasping one of the aged oak's drooping branches. As he held on, George broke through the lake water near him and John extended his hand. George grabbed it as John helped him kick his way to his own nearby branch.

Lou's laughter could be heard above. "John, if you drown do I get your room?"

"Not funny Lou! Just...oh no, the map!" John thrust his hand inside his inside vest pocket and held the map, which was wrapped in cloth, above the water. "Take it, Lou. Unwrap it and dry it on your dress, hurry!"

Lou bent down to take the map. She swiftly unwrapped the dripping cloth and pat-dried the old paper on the frill of her dress. "It's just a little smeared – but I think it's okay!"

"Good," said John. "What happened, anyway?"

"We fell," said George, still gasping.

"*We* didn't," said John, also breathing hard while

floating in the cool lake. "You did and then I tried to save you and that made me fall!"

"But – "

"Never mind that," John said, "why did Owen leave so fast?"

"I don't know. I saw him look that way and…" George looked over John's shoulder, out into the lake. "What…what is that?" George began.

John's eyes adjusted and stared out toward the middle of the water. The sun was low and the shadows were thick. But in the subdued light of the lake there was no mistaking it. A huge, curved hump emerged from the water. As it moved the hump dipped below the surface of the lake. In its place, a long serpent-like neck emerged. The creature was swimming toward them.

"Go! Go!" John yelled.

Both boys sloshed and swam their way to the shore while Lou moved as quickly as possible down the oak toward its base. John chanced a look behind him, even as he arrived on shore. The long neck of the creature bent down, completely submerging in water. As it did, a hump rose up behind it at the same time. It was still coming.

"Faster!" yelled John.

"Come on, hurry!" yelled Lou who had already made it to shore.

As John and George reached land they looked back.

The lake creature had also changed direction. It turned, as if to follow the boys. It moved toward them in the water while John, George and Lou ran on land.

With firm land beneath their feet, the three of them blurred across the edge of the lake until they reached the lip of the mountain. Without a backward glance, they slipped over the great forested hill in descent.

Chapter 10

The Admiral

September 22, 1759
(69 years ago)

The French admiral stood straight as an arrow on the bow of his ship, peering onto the shoreline of Lake Ontario. Now, just as the day's light ascended, was when he felt most at home on his vessel. His men knew to leave him alone while he gathered his thoughts. Usually he would make his way to his cabin now to write. But not this evening. He did not want to lose the setting before him. The admiral sat down and picked up his quill and began to write.

Dear Annette,

I am sorry for this distance between letters, but circumstances have intervened more than once. The British choke off our trading channels at every opportunity. It is a maddening war. I told you in an earlier letter that we lost Fort Niagara this summer to the British and abandoned Fort Rouillé at Toronto.

A few weeks ago, in port, I was made an admiral. There was little formality, not like it would have been in France, had I been home. I would like to think of this as a show of confidence and yet I know how many men we have lost to battle, disease and despair. I fear I am but the latest choice and I have no illusions about being divinely different from those who have come before me. However, I do harbour hope that I shall outlast this war and be with you soon.

How lovely the land is here! As I write this, we have been lying low along the shore of Lake Ontario between Kingston and York in a land of bays the British have dubbed Prince Edward County. For now, I have directed most of the fleet further into Lake Ontario while we explore here.

I have a French map created just two years ago and it has been some help. Although, realistically, this is Indian country after all, no matter what either we or the British say.

I am astonished by the bay we have sailed into. Rising up before me as I pen these words is a magnificent hill, heavily wooded and green with promise. From the hill, a wide waterfall careens over the side and makes its way to the bay down a crooked stream.

For the moment, we are in a holding position and I feel that I must explore it, provided it appears safe to do so. I do not think the British have any real numbers of men here. As much as I love the open water, it will be good to feel the land beneath my feet for awhile.

I think of you often and I hope each day that I will be home with you soon.

With all my love,

Joseph Fortin

Chapter 11

Devil's Lake

Supper was awkward. Before splitting up to go home, John, George and Lou had agreed to remain silent about what they had seen. Instead, John had said they had simply fallen in the lake after having gotten into a good natured shoving match with one another. John took the mild scolding compared to the alternative of being banned from the lake.

But why would he ever want to go back anyway? He tried to focus on dinner. What he had seen less than an hour ago would not leave his mind. Anxious sweat trickled down his right temple and he brushed it away. He tried to tune in to the conversation.

"How are you faring these days?" asked Helen.

"Oh, the ague knocks me down sometimes," said the colonel, "but I just keep getting up again."

"What's ague?" asked Lou.

"Chills and sometimes fever," said Helen. "I imagine it's not pleasant."

The colonel waved his hand to dismiss any more talk about his health. "Never mind me. Kingston's in a fine mess right now."

Helen nodded. "It's the typhoid, isn't it? We heard from Cornelius."

He nodded grimly. "Seems like it's everywhere. So far we've been untouched. I'm glad to see you're all doing well here."

John knew typhoid was a terrible disease, which often began with high fevers and diarrhoea so severe it often resulted in death.

"How's Allan these days?" Helen asked, referring to the colonel's grown son.

Colonel Macpherson shook his head in disbelief. "You know Allan – he's the social point for the whole clan up there in Napanee – ever since he built that big home. He's doing mighty well for himself."

A long silence occurred and John sensed they were no longer thinking about typhoid or the colonel's son. When the colonel and Hugh Macdonald sat at the same table, supper was bound to end up being tense. They always had to get through the same conversation they had been having for years.

"How's the flour-milling business, Hugh?" asked the colonel. He was an intimidating figure in his full uniform, sitting stiffly and cutting his last piece of venison with precision. His trim, silver moustache moved with his chewing.

"Couldn't be better," said Hugh. He dug into his last bite of boiled potato.

More silence. John concentrated on the three bunches of onions and herbs drying from the ceiling beams as he chewed, not fully there. He was nearly finished anyway.

"You know, I don't know why you ever left good old Kingston," said Lieutenant Colonel Macpherson. "It has what anyone needs."

"I remember – except for customers," said Hugh.

"Maybe that had to do with how things were run."

Hugh, who had changed careers several times, including as a shopkeeper in Kingston, put his fork down and looked at the colonel. Helen got up to get the teapot from the trivet on the counter, bustling more than usual as if to put distance between her and the conversation.

"Why are you here, Donald?" asked Hugh. "The news sheet? There's no printer in Stone Mills so I don't know where it's coming from."

The colonel raised an eyebrow. "This goes beyond a news sheet. Other things are happening – things which I'm not at liberty to talk about. Let's just say there's good reason to be vigilant."

John watched his father stab a green bean. "I'm not even saying I agree with the things we're reading in the news, Donald, but you have to admit the Reformers have come up with a big win in the election earlier this year. There's a clear majority of them in the Assembly now in York – including Mackenzie."

The colonel bristled. "Poppycock. That fool won't last, mark my words. What sort of man wants the chaos of American-style democracy?"

"The same sort who are tired of being treated unfairly, I suppose Donald," said Hugh.

John cleared his throat. "Mrs. Pringle...er, Miss Pringle says that if the Family Compact doesn't like a decision made by the elected Assembly, they can just overrule it. She said that's why some people want a change. Is that true, Colonel?"

The colonel wiped his moustache. "Miss Pringle... isn't she the widow at the general store?"

John nodded.

"Well, that's true my boy. But those rules are there for a reason. It's a dangerous thing to let just any common man have enough power to make decisions without a sober, educated voice of reason. Sometimes the common man doesn't always know what's good for him."

The colonel chewed more aggressively. "Let me be clear about William Lyon Mackenzie," he continued. "This is the greatest fool Scotland has ever produced. In fact, I'm even sorry that he is a Scot."

John exchanged glances with Moll. Mackenzie was considered a huge thorn in the ruling party's side. There wasn't a Tory alive who didn't wish he would just disappear. Some people believed he might one day incite a rebellion if he didn't stop.

Three years ago, Mackenzie published a newspaper called the *Colonial Advocate* which talked openly about changing the way government worked and breaking up the monopoly of power the Tories held. Mackenzie even wanted to unite the British colonies, which John thought was unlikely.

John remembered hearing that Mackenzie once attacked the Tories so strongly in his newspaper that two years ago, young members of the Tories smashed his printing press. Since then, it seemed as if he was more famous than ever.

Hugh devoured another boiled potato and smiled in edgy amusement at the table talk. He allowed a brief grin at John before he looked at the colonel again.

"You know what Mackenzie says – "every free government must have two parties, a governing party and a party in check. What do you think of that Donald?"

The colonel wiped his mouth with his napkin. "You can call me Colonel."

A shout outside caught everyone's attention. Hugh cocked his head and partially stood. More hollering from other voices could be heard.

"What the devil…?" said Hugh. Wiping his mouth with his handkerchief, he strode to the front window

and looked outside. He was followed by the colonel and
Helen. John, Moll and Lou filled the viewing crevices
left between the leaning, grown-ups' bodies.

John could see Peter and Charlotte Goslin, a farming
couple from the top of Lake on the Mountain. They
were both speaking loudly and other men and women
from the village were gathering around them.

The Macdonald's and the colonel all rushed outside
into the dusk. Nearly half the village was already there.
Big Solomon Brook's red hair and beard could be seen
standing high amongst the crowd. The smiling farmer,
Darius Marshall, was just walking up to the crowd and
stood near Hannah Pringle. John also noticed five or six
farmers he recognized from both below and above the
mountain.

"What's going on?" Hugh demanded. A chorus of
voices continued to talk at once.

"Silence!" yelled the colonel. The retired officer
stepped forward. The round smudge of evening sun set
his uniform's gold buttons alight. Within seconds the
crowd had hushed.

"Now," said the colonel. "What is this about?"

Peter Goslin cleared his throat. "There's something
living in that lake up there – we saw it with our own
eyes!" Charlotte Goslin nodded, her eyes wet with fear.

John and Lou looked at each other. Lou was obviously biting her tongue and John subtly shook his head so

she'd keep quiet. He could feel a bead of sweat creep under his hairline.

Should they tell everyone what they saw, too?

"It's not just Whisky Wilson, you know," said Peter. "There's something…grotesque in that lake. Something terrible."

"I told you! I told you all!" shrieked a skinny, haggard man. Whisky Wilson popped out of the crowd like a grubby leprechaun and began dancing a short jig in front of everyone. A few people gently pushed him out of the way where he continued his dance off to the side of the crowd.

"But it's not just that," said Peter. "We found this on our way down here. I'm pretty sure it's Anson Rightmyer's."

Those who could see clearly gasped. It was a blood-soaked, torn shirt.

"He was supposed to come by yesterday to help with the harvest and he never showed."

Hannah Pringle put her hand to her mouth. "He's right," she said, getting closer to the shirt. "It's from my store. Anson bought that shirt last summer." The crowd erupted into noises of confirmation.

"Attention!" yelled the colonel. He stood straighter, which John thought was impossible. "We are going to handle this in a civilized way."

The crowd buzzed quietly while a short, stocky man

parted them as he walked. "A wonderful idea, colonel. I will certainly be as civilized as possible as we figure this out."

The colonel stiffened as the barrel-chested man moved forward. Constable Charles Ogden had a thick band of brown hair encircling his head although he was nearly bald on top. A substantial brown moustache angled down around his mouth.

"Ahh, Constable," said the colonel. "I defer to your local knowledge."

John saw his father smirk as the colonel was put in his place.

"Well thank you kindly," said the constable without kindness in his voice. "Now what's going on?"

Lewis Patterson, another farmer, spoke up first. "Anson Rightmyer has been missing for two days and at the same time more and more folks have been seeing some kind of abomination in that lake," he said, pointing to the top of the mountain. "Some kind of an evil serpent. And now we find Anson's bloody shirt? This village isn't safe anymore."

The crowd buzzed in chatter with many people nodding their heads in agreement. John realized he would have to tell someone, something, about what they had seen.

"Hold on, hold on," said the constable. He rubbed his bald head and looked at Peter Goslin. "Where exactly did you find Mr. Rightmyer's shirt – in the woods? Near his home?"

"No sir," said Peter. "We found it on the edge of the Devil's lake itself. Right where we saw the serpent – in Lake on the Mountain."

Constable Ogden used his forearm to wipe his brow. "First thing tomorrow morning I'm going to want to talk with anyone who's seen something in that lake. I have my doubts about these stories, but I'll hear anyone out."

A few voices erupted to argue and then John raised his hand. He made eye contact with Constable Ogden. "We did, sir – we saw the serpent."

Chapter 12

The Lake Effect

Constable Charles Ogden never wanted to be a constable. Who would? The money was poor and the rewards were almost none. Up until now, the most action he had ever had in the job was impounding three horses someone found wandering along the edge of the village.

As he swished his morning tea around in his cup his wife busied herself in the background of their modest home. Living only a quarter mile from the centre of Stone Mills, he was generally in a good position to keep an eye on the community, both below and above the mountain.

Oh, he knew something more difficult was bound to happen on his watch. That's just the way things are. He would never have suspected this, though – not in a hundred years. The whole village was going mad. Lake serpents! And now he had a missing person and a bloody shirt was found.

Constable Ogden was interviewing each and every

person who had claimed to have seen this lake serpent. He surveyed the faces of the two boys in front of him, John Macdonald and George Cloutier. Both had been involved in their fair share of mischief – especially the Macdonald boy – but only of the typical variety for this age. Apparently John's younger sister had been there, too, but Hugh Macdonald had wanted to spare her any more talk of lake serpents. The younger ones were prone to nightmares and he couldn't blame him for wanting to leave her out of this.

The constable glanced over at Hugh who was nervously smoothing his large moustache beside them. Seeing Hugh Macdonald made him think about Lieutenant Colonel Macpherson again. What was a retired British colonel doing in his village anyway, other than visiting family? He had never liked the colonel. He always got the impression from him that he had little time for common folk.

"Now when you say 'lake serpent' just exactly what might you mean by that?" asked the constable.

John and George looked at one another. Hugh nodded, urging them to get to the point.

"It was getting dark, sir, Constable Ogden," began John. "But what we saw seemed to have two humps and a long, snake-like neck."

Hugh fidgeted. "Like he said, Charles, it was dark. Could have been anything, right? I didn't even know about this until John told everyone last night, after Peter Goslin's story."

The constable looked at John who was clearly irked at the lack of belief from his father.

"Are you saying you think they imagined it completely?" the constable asked.

"No, I'm not saying that, Charles. But a lake serpent? It seems..." his voice trailed off.

"Crazy?" the constable finished.

"Yes – crazy as can be," said Hugh.

The constable drank the rest of his tea and set it on the table. Within a few seconds his wife had cleared the cup and began to wash it.

"The trouble is, Hugh, these boys aren't the first now, are they?"

"I suppose not," said Hugh.

"And it's not just old Wilson we're talking about either, as you know," said Constable Ogden. "In addition to the Goslin's, who we just heard from, William Blair also said he saw something when he was fishing that he couldn't explain. A long neck, then humps moving through the water. He was so sure of what he saw that he left his fishing pole and even his farm. He loaded what he could on a large bateau and hitched a ride off to Kingston. That was just two weeks ago. You knew that."

Hugh nodded. "Just thought there had to be another

reason – that Blair was exaggerating, was all."

"And the thing is," said the constable, "it's always the same description of this thing, too. Not sure how I account for that." Hugh said nothing.

"And Frank and Eleanor Eddy were taking an evening walk near the lake when both of them felt there were moving shadows across the lake at first, then a long neck and head. She wants to move to York and he's not sure at this point."

John and George looked at each other in tight-lipped vindication.

"The interesting thing is that it was either evening or night when folks said they saw this thing."

Hugh folded his hands in front of him. "Do you know how terrible this is for business, Charles? If the farmers around the lake end up moving away how am I supposed to make a living?"

He shook his head. "It's not good for anyone's business, Hugh, except maybe mine, eh? But I sure don't need the adventure."

The constable got up to stretch. What was he supposed to tell the high constable about this? Not that he'd care, sitting in his office in Kingston, he mused. Nobody cared about what happened in the small villages of Upper Canada except the villagers themselves.

He'd have to take matters into his own hands. Devil's lake indeed.

Chapter 13

Democracy is Coming

Moll smoothed her dress, deep in thought, as she made her way to the general store. Her woven basket hung in the crook of her arm. The porcelain-skinned girl looked out at the bay and watched the aging sunrise leak over the water. A flock of birds lifted in unison and flew into the sun, as if propelled by an urgent request.

There was a quiet sense of alarm in the village today. Moll could feel it. People were worried about the safety of their families and for their businesses. She was anxious, too. She didn't want to leave Stone Mills. Like John, she believed their father would move them if business began to suffer. She wondered what it was like for John and George right now, having to meet Constable Ogden first thing this morning. She wondered what they could have possibly seen.

As Pringle's General Store grew closer she made a mental note to have Lou help her gather more greens from the garden before the rodents took everything.

Moll glanced up at the lit, wooded mountain rising up behind their home and the mill. Strange, how whatever was living in that lake was only appearing now.

She was also worried about her brother. Last night she had heard him through the walls of her room, obviously dreaming something terrible. She wondered if it was about little James. Or maybe the lake serpent...or both? He wouldn't talk about it though. Boys were odd at the best of times and her brother was no different.

Moll took in the dark, brown of the two-storey general store with its yawning porch. Out back, a long, twisted storage shed was in need of repair. Climbing the steps of the store she could see the tilted handwriting of Hannah Pringle. The note read 'back in a moment.'

She gathered her dress underneath her and sat on the porch and waited. Moll desperately needed a bolt of dark green cloth to finish sewing the quilts Mother had asked her to prepare for the fall. As well, they were almost out of tea and brown sugar. That wouldn't do with the colonel here visiting.

After five minutes had passed Moll peered into the window on the front door but didn't see any movement. Thinking Miss Pringle might be out back, Moll set out to find her. There was no sign of anyone. She was about to return to the front when she noticed the door of the back storage shed was slightly ajar. Moll made her way to the old shed.

For some reason her heart was racing and she tried to take longer, deeper breaths. As she reached out to push the door, she thought she could hear someone inside.

"Miss Pri –?" she began.

"Oh!" Hannah Pringle held her arm up in self-protection seeing Moll's outstretched hand about to push the door open. Moll jumped back and held her racing heart. "I'm sorry, Miss Pringle. You sure scared me," said Moll.

Hannah, looking very much like Moll, with one hand over her heart, nodded and shut the storage shed door behind her. "That makes two of us, young miss. I'm sorry if I was longer than anticipated."

She touched her hair, ensuring it was still in place. "What can I do for you today?" she asked. She glided back to the front porch as she spoke. Moll admired her rose-coloured, summer dress. Then she wondered if Miss Pringle would ever look for another husband or just remain a spinster.

"Just a bolt of dark green cloth, Miss. Pringle," said Moll. "And a little tea and sugar."

"I'm fresh out of dark green but there's this dark blue shade here, or a lovely rich brown," said Hannah, holding up the cloth.

Moll pictured the quilts for the fall at their house. "I'll take the brown, then, thank you."

Hannah was someone Moll had long admired.

Perhaps it was her independence she found so attractive. As Hannah began to measure the brown sugar, Moll could see a streak of black on the right side of her neck.

"Miss Pringle…you have a long, black mark – here," said Moll moving toward her and pointing to her own neck.

"Oh – thank you," she said, backing up from Moll and nearly tripping. "I can get it with a rag in the back. In fact, why don't you just write down what you need to take here," she said, pushing a ledger forward on the counter. "I'll simply put it on your tab. Yes, that will work just fine," she said, answering for Moll. "Take care now."

"But…"

The store owner rushed into the back room and closed the door, leaving Moll to finish shopping for herself.

***

Darius Marshall sat on a wooden stool facing Anson Rightmyer. He gently stroked the back of the feeble sparrow with his thumb and hummed. He had noticed the bird struggling to fly last week, its left wing in distress – likely from a larger bird. It might need some extra attention and rest before it could fly again.

His eyes drifted to a copy of the news sheet which questioned the politics of the Tories. It was perfect timing, he had to admit. He wished he had made it himself. But whoever the printer was, he was grateful for the man's timing.

Looking up, Darius smiled at the shirtless Anson Rightmyer. He didn't want it to be this way and yet his men were overly protective. He tried to broaden it beyond the grin that was usually plastered across his face. As he stared at the sweat beading on Anson's forehead, he wondered what it was that separated a killer from a kidnapper. Courage? Caution?

Darius straightened his back, then stood and leaned against the cabin's rough wall to consider his own question. In the past, he had been trained to kill as a soldier and would do so again if the situation suited him. For now, that would accelerate plans too swiftly. The wandering, nine-fingered farmer had gotten too close for his own good. Darius and his men had no choice but to take action.

The others moved like cougars in the forest, as he had once done, always aware of their prey, always committed to victory.

Darius knew he was out of practice compared to the eight, younger men who worked for him. And yet they respected him for past glories. They were allowing him to once again lead them because Darius told them he was on a secret mission with the backing of U.S. President John Quincy Adams.

He was going to bring democracy to this sad, pathetic colony. A colony that took so much from its people. Just as the Family Compact drove him out of York. Just like one of these same godless men stole his wife, Sophia. He would bring the one thing the Tories could not deal with – a complete loss of control.

He and Sophia had moved to York after the 'incident,' as he liked to call it. With a great deal of practice, they had shed their Kentuckian accents and took their place in Upper Canadian society. Ironic, wasn't it? He had fought so hard against British North America, only to end up living among them.

But Sophia hated York. It was too rough for her sensibilities, no matter what Darius tried to do. She blamed him for the downturn her life had taken.

And that's when Edgar had shown up, born and bred into the Family Compact. A smug, rich Brit with a sense of entitlement, if ever there was one. He and Sophia had met at a dance they had all attended. Within a month, she had declared she was leaving him for Edgar.

Darius bit into his tongue as he remembered the humiliation. That was when he left York and wandered into Stone Mills, numb and alone. The setting soothed him. There were tongues of land formed by the endless arms of the Bay of Quinte. The massive trees and the great hill, capped by an unexplainable lake. For awhile, this life was all he needed or wanted.

But then the people started opening their mouths. He had to hear their stupid British thoughts and their stupid British rules. They were all the same as Edgar, he soon decided. Cheaters, liars, and followers of the king.

Had he not fought against this? Had he not lifted a long gun against this way of living? He knew he had to return to his roots and fight for democracy. These Brits might not appreciate it now. But their children would, when they had a chance to grow up free.

Over in York, Mackenzie was perhaps the only one who understood how important it was to work against the Family Compact. He had the heart of a true American beating in him. He would love to meet him someday. Mackenzie's newspaper and other upstarts like the *Stone Mills Reformer* would help him in his quest to bring real democracy to Upper Canada.

Darius watched Anson's eyes flit to the left and then the right. The captive man's brow grew thick with sweat and Darius felt the shadows behind him flinch. Two of his men had returned to the hidden cabin. He turned toward them slightly as he set the sparrow down on the table.

"I'm glad to see he's alive," said Darius.

"Why?" asked one shadow. "He's no one."

"It's not time," said Darius. "We'll keep them guessing for now. The bloodied shirt will only increase the anxiety." Anson's breathing was rapid and shallow behind his gag.

"What about the British colonel?" asked the other shadow. "You saw him arrive."

Darius shrugged. "Of course I did. He's merely an unwanted family member, dropping in to see the Macdonald's. He isn't a concern."

"He's not the only Macdonald who's a concern. The boy has been poking around over here, too."

"Oh, I doubt he'll be back."

"And if he – or his Brit uncle – keeps it up?"

"Then we will deal with them decisively."

Darius stared at the pleading eyes of his neighbour. He began to realize his men were growing crazy with wait. He suddenly realized that if he left Anson alone here for more than a few hours at a time he'd likely be a dead man. The only thing to determine now was whether or not he cared.

Chapter 14

The Constable's Search

Constable Charles Ogden dug his feet into the main trail that laced the side of the mountain. Halfway up the great, wooded hill he had to stop and rest, pulling a tattered handkerchief out of his pocket. He wiped the sweat from the back of his thick neck and the top of his bald head. Looking back at his progress, he sighed and continued his ascent.

Even with the sun in free fall, dipping toward the horizon, it was still warm this evening – too warm to be out looking for make-believe lake serpents. Oh, he believed folks were seeing something. Probably the play of shadows on the surface or maybe some large, oddly-shaped driftwood floating about.

He didn't bring his rifle so as not to alarm anyone. He didn't want to give villagers the impression he was even entertaining the notion that something might be amiss in their strange, little lake.

The constable walked past the bent oak tree where

the Macdonald and Cloutier boys had said they were playing. There was a greater density of trees nearby and thicker brush. Give it time, though, and this side of the lake would be developed, too. A farming family could pretty much count on clearing about four acres per year for crops. It wouldn't take too long.

He was also near Anson Rightmyer's farm. It was indeed odd that no one had seen Anson in days. Did he go to see his brother over in Demorestville? He didn't make that trip often, though. Anson was usually a constant in town, either chatting up Hugh Macdonald at the mill or trying to hang around Hannah at the general store. Probably lonely, ever since Mary Ann had died. Bless her soul for keeping the fool alive all those years.

Anson's bloody shirt had to mean something but he wasn't sure what. The truth is the man had always been accident prone. But if he had injured himself very badly then that didn't explain how his shirt could end up by the lake.

He looked out into the still water and tried to imagine something large enough to pull a grown man into the lake and eat him alive.

Ridiculous.

Approaching the shore, the constable crouched down and studied the sand near the edge of the water. He saw that the area had been recently disturbed. For all he knew, though, it could have been the Macdonald and

Cloutier boys, since he wasn't far from the bent oak tree. The constable watched the water bugs swim in circles for a moment then pivoted on his heel and prepared to return home.

As he took a step, the surface of the water was punctured. He turned and saw a circle of ripples in the water further out into the lake. The constable held his breath.

Fish. Should come back here with a pole some night, once this village is calmed down.

He turned to walk home but then saw movement in his peripheral vision. Glancing back at the shadowed lake again, his lips parted. A great shadow rose from the lake itself. A thick, snake-like neck arced into the air and the constable squinted at what he was seeing.

"What the devil..."

The constable backed up a step and felt his feet leave the ground completely. A cold hand over his mouth was the last thing he recalled before blacking out.

Chapter 15

A Greater Good

After supper, John ran for the edge of the Bay of Quinte. He looked around for George who was supposed to meet him but he hadn't yet arrived. John worked his fingers deeply underneath a small, wedged rock while he waited. He pried the flattened stone from the ground and knocked off the remaining dirt.

Round and smooth. Perfect.

He bent his knees and looked out onto the calm, evening water. The village was quiet today, in a peculiar sort of way. It hadn't even been that busy at the mill. John sucked in the moist air and watched the sunlight play across the water. Then he cocked his hand back with his prized stone.

"If I were you I'd get a bit lower."

John jumped and spun around. He dropped the flat rock and watched it land on its edge, rolling toward the feet of Darius Marshall. The man bent down and picked it up, palming it as if to weigh its worthiness.

"I do apologize, young man. Didn't mean to startle you."

John felt his racing heart slow down at seeing the grinning farmer. "That's alright, Mr. Marshall. "I'm surprised I didn't hear you. I'm just waiting for my friend, George."

"I tend to tread lightly – an old habit from my soldiering days."

"You were a soldier?"

He nodded, handing the rock back to John. "Yes siree. Don't talk about it much, really."

"So you fought against the Americans in the War of 1812 then?" John asked.

Darius flinched. "Oh, yes. We have to support king and country, we do."

John nodded. He bent his knees again and prepared to throw, glancing back at Darius who smiled his approval at John's stance. Or at least John thought he did. He couldn't tell that his face changed much, other than an eyebrow twitch.

"You're from York, right?" John asked. "How'd you wind up in Stone Mills, Mr. Marshall?"

"Came here to get away from the crowds," said Darius. "Now tell me, young man, is that a relative visiting – the officer?"

"Yes, sir. Lieutenant Colonel Donald Macpherson – my uncle from Kingston."

"He seems a bit on the older side to be in the army."

"He's retired."

"He's not acting retired."

Darius bent and threw a stone in one motion. John counted eight skips.

"Nice throw, Mr. Marshall. I guess you're right about the colonel – that's what we all call him. I'm not sure why he's here, really, but Father thinks it has to do with the news sheet that's been floating around."

"Ahh – yes, I've seen it. And what do you think of it?" Darius asked.

"I think it stirs up everybody and that can't be good."

"Why?"

John shrugged. He scuffled around for another stone. "I don't know – it just seems like it gets people all riled up."

Darius polished another stone. "Well, that's the point young man. When government tries to tell you what you can and can't do, it can get to you. Makes people a little crazy. That's another reason why I left York."

"I don't understand," said John.

"The Family Compact."

"You mean the Tories?"

Darius laughed. "I like the term Family Compact better – William Lyon Mackenzie came up with that you know."

John nodded. "Yes sir, my father told me. Miss

Pringle talked to George and me about this too."

"Did she now? That's a mighty smart woman over there." They both looked in the direction of the general store. John noticed that Darius' eyes lingered a bit longer in her direction.

The man brushed a few stray, thinning strands of brown hair the wind had blown in front of his eyes. "Well, young man, maybe this Mackenzie will one day lead some kind of revolution, like they had in the U.S. What do you think of that?" Darius flung his stone. Five skips.

"Meaning no disrespect, sir, but I think there must be other ways to figure out how to run our affairs, other than having a war."

John whipped the small stone. Six skips.

The farmer scratched his head and took a half step closer to John. "War is all we have left when freedom falters, son. Sometimes that's when a greater good comes calling." John stared at him quizzically.

"What I'm saying is," Darius added, "maybe some folks will end up choosing to join up with our friends to the south. Then we'd be left with just one country, at least for the northern half of the continent."

John laughed at the thought. "And what country would it be then?"

Darius' eyes narrowed. "The U.S., of course. It's larger – it could absorb these colonies just fine.

Speaking theoretically, young man." He tapped his head. "Keeps the mind sharp."

John considered the idea for a brief moment as he kicked for another stone with the ball of his foot. "No one from around here would want to join the United States, Mr. Marshall. Even the people who used to be Americans came here because they wanted to remain British. That's how the Adolphustown area was settled, when Peter Van Alstine and some of the United Empire Loyalists left the U.S. and landed here. It was June 16th, 1784 – every kid in the county knows that date."

Darius was silent as he stared off in the distance.

"Mr. Marshall? It's funny but I can't figure out your accent. Where did you say you were from, originally?"

Darius pointed to a small figure moving toward the bay from the middle of the village. "Here comes your friend now."

John squinted. "Wow, your eyes are good Mr. Marshall. You're right."

George began to run and reached the edge of the bay a few moments later.

"Hi George – you remember Mr. Marshall, right?" John turned to reintroduce them. No one was there.

Chapter 16

As Mean as They Come

John grabbed the side of the bateau and helped Cornelius edge the *Morning Bloom* onto the shore. The lean boatman's hands blurred as he tied the slender boat to its post, something he must have done thousands of times, John figured.

Cornelius stepped over the side onto the bank and dragged his bad leg a few steps, under the mid-morning sun. He looked at a small pile of flour sacks on the ground. "That's it?" He looked from Hugh Macdonald to John. "Is there more coming?"

Hugh shook his head. "No – afraid not."

Cornelius whistled. "It's the bloody lake creature, isn't it? I've heard the rumours even in the other villages. Hard to imagine people are just up and leaving their crops."

John swallowed and stared at his feet at the mention of the creature. He hated the fact that thinking about the lake – and what they had seen in it – made him feel so anxious. Before Hugh or John could say anything they turned to the sound of an approaching wagon. Nathaniel Pitman, the massive saw mill operator, drove his large team of horses toward them.

"John, if you wouldn't mind?" Cornelius gestured to the few sacks of flour to load in the bateau.

"You don't care for Mr. Pitman, do you?" asked John in a quiet voice. They heaved the sack onto the lip of the boat. He glanced over at the massive, dark-haired figure perched on top of the wagon.

Cornelius sniffed. "The man's mean, John – as mean as they come. I saw him reduce one of his employees to tears one time a couple of years ago when they were un-loading in this very same place – a grown man."

The two large bay horses halted.

"Nathaniel." Hugh nodded.

The man grunted. Without a clear word he unhitched the ties around the cut planks of wood in the back of his wagon. Like his father's flour sacks, it seemed to John that it was a far cry from what he might normally send to Kingston.

"That's it, then?" asked Cornelius.

Nathaniel's dark, brown eyes trained on Cornelius. "Just load it."

***

John drew George aside. "I want to know what the colonel is up to."

The bay was choppy and moody and mirrored the sky over Stone Mills. John, George, Moll and Lou were having an outside dinner just a few feet away from the bay. Dark, grey waves pushed toward the shore and splashed over a large crag of rock. John closed his eyes as he leaned back on the scruff of grass and sand. He let the spray wash over his face.

George's eyes bulged. "You mean, you want to spy on your uncle?"

"I wouldn't call it spying," said John. "I just want to watch him without him knowing."

George looked at Moll. "Moll, how would you define the word spying?"

She laughed and John affably shoved his friend. "Listen, I heard he went to the top of the mountain and I want to see if he's at Mr. Pitman's."

George chomped on a carrot while he let John's words sink in. "You want to go to the lake – after what we saw? Are you crazy, mon ami?"

John shook his head. "No way – not the lake, really." John felt his palms grow sweaty. "Not that close. We can just stay near the edge of the mountain – I want to peek into the saw mill and see if the colonel is there. I think something's up there, but I don't know what. He's hardly talked to me since he got here, which is odd."

"I told you last time I do not want to go near the saw mill, either," said George, pacing. "Nobody listens to me."

"I listen to you, George." Lou was wandering along the shore line of the bay but took time to look up and smile at George.

John ignored his little sister. "It's daytime," John reminded him. "That...thing we saw in the lake has only been seen in the evening. Look, I'm worried Father is going to follow the lead of some of the other villagers and leave."

In fact he had just seen evidence of it this morning, when Cornelius loaded the bateau with half the amount of flour he usually picked up in Stone Mills. It wasn't a good sign.

"Maybe that thing is nocturnal," said Moll. "And that's why people see it only at night?"

John nodded. "Maybe."

Moll looked thoughtful. "But John, what does Colonel Macpherson have to do with the people leaving – or Mr. Pitman, for that matter?"

John shrugged and began to pace. The sides of his hair sprung out in the wind as he walked. "I'm not sure. Just a feeling that he's looking into this. And remember, Constable Ogden said he was going up there last night. Maybe he and the colonel are working together?"

"It did not seem like they were friends," said George.

He chose one of the crusts of bread Moll had packed and sat, cross-legged, near Moll. "And why aren't we looking for treasure, John? That sounds more exciting to me."

"We will," said John, feeling his inside pocket where the map remained. He had been so disturbed by the lake serpent they had seen that he hadn't been able to think about much else – other than maybe his father packing the family up and leaving Stone Mills. John pointed to the flour mill. "Look."

Everyone looked at the mill. One farmer standing beside a small horse cart waited his turn. George shrugged. "What?"

"At this time of year, there should be a line-up past Pringle's Store. On wagons, horseback – farmers' backs – they should be hauling in the wheat right now. It should be non-stop flour milling for us," said John.

Moll nodded and George sighed. "So if everyone is either running away from Stone Mills because they're scared of the lake creature…" began Moll.

"I'm not scared," John lied.

"…or even just distracted, not tending their fields on time because of this, then Father's business is in big trouble," she finished.

No one said anything. "And you know what that means," Moll added.

"We'll be moving again," said Lou, drifting into the

conversation.

"George, do you want me to go back to Kingston knowing our father's business is growing worse every day, when it should be busy?" asked John. "We'd likely move and I'd never see you again."

Lou jumped up and patted George's shoulder. "You should listen to my brother – today he's making sense."

George sighed and grabbed a second carrot. "If I go, then it is not near the lake, right?"

"No lake," John assured. "Just the forest on the edges of the mountain where I bet the colonel is searching. Mr. Rightmyer was eaten in the lake – we'll stay away from there."

Moll shook her head. "They only found his shirt, John."

"Yes, with blood on it," said John. "And I wonder why?" He made a serpent's neck with his arm and used his hand to make a mouth, snapping at the air.

George laughed uneasily. "But what about the treasure? If we use our time on the map we could become rich. Or, if we use our time spying on your uncle and Mr. Pitman, we could be jailed."

"It's not a choice, George – we'll do both. But if we don't figure out what's going on, our time in Stone Mills is limited. Father likes to move around too much – we've always lived with a sense of uncertainty about that. I don't want to give him an excuse."

George pulled out a scratched pocket watch. "We still have an hour before I have to go home and you have to work in the mill. Are you coming with us Moll?"

Moll stood and brushed herself off. "You two go on ahead. I have sewing to do."

John pointed at Lou discretely so Moll would notice, as his eyes bulged out. "Oh, and I need your help, Lou," said Moll, understanding.

"But I want to go with them!" said Lou as John mouthed 'no' behind her and held up his hands in a mock prayer.

"Maybe next time," said Moll. "We have to figure out what's for supper tonight, too."

"I want to be a boy." Lou stomped off toward the house and John tried to refrain from smiling too much.

"Thanks Moll – and thanks for dinner," said John.

"I'm keeping track," she said, following Lou. "The tab's getting high, John."

"Sisters," said John, shaking his head. He took a deep breath and turned to George. "Okay. Let's go."

***

John and George dissolved into the woods behind the flour mill and clawed their way up the flat-topped mountain. Sunlight filtered through the dense trees and left bright scars of light on the ground. Scrabbling over the edge, they ran the short distance to the edge of the lake which was now bathed in the hot, midday sun. They stopped to eye the shores.

"Mon ami...isn't that your uncle right there?" George pointed to a figure kneeling down at the south side of the lake. John cupped his eyes to block the sunlight.

"Yes, that's him. No one else would be wearing a full military uniform around here. But what's he doing?"

They walked toward the colonel, John stealing glances at the lake to his right. It was placid. Still. As they got closer, the older officer noticed them and stood straight. He smoothed his uniform and looked around.

"And how may I help you two today?" he asked. His silver moustache twitched when he spoke. Somehow the colonel always made John feel like he had to report on something, as if he were a soldier.

"Um, nothing sir. That is, we don't need any help at all. We're just exploring," said John.

"I dare say I can't imagine what for," said the colonel.

John glanced at George with a 'help me now' look.

"Treasure!" George burst out.

"Treasure?" The colonel laughed. It seemed to put his mind at ease. His face softened and his eyes looked wistful. "When I was a young boy, growing up in England, I used to listen to my father tell me stories about the Welshman, Henry Morgan. He was a pirate in the Caribbean islands you know."

He sighed. "Before I got older and wiser I used to think about treasure, too. Can't cause any harm, I suppose."

"Are you investigating something, sir?" John asked.

There. He had just come right out and asked it.

The colonel's face darkened but he didn't answer. He looked across the lake as he asked, "Have any of you seen Constable Ogden since yesterday evening?"

John swallowed. "No sir. The last we heard he was going to search the lake area last night. After Mr. Rightmyer disappeared and all."

The colonel nodded. "Yes – except he didn't return home to his wife last night."

John and George exchanged worried looks. "First, Mr. Rightmyer and now, Constable Ogden," John said.

The colonel stiffened. John had never seen his uncle look so worried. "You best run along boys. Ta ta, now."

John bumped George and they began to back away, toward the lip of the mountain.

"And John?"

"Yes sir?" said John, spinning around.

"I'll be recommending to your mother and father that you best stay away from Lake on the Mountain. You, too, George. And if I can't get some answers in the next two days, I'll recommend that we evacuate the entire village."

Chapter 17

Lake of the Gods

September 24, 1759
(69 years ago)

Deep into the forest the admiral wandered as brooding elms extended their arms to slow his progress. Pulling branches aside, he stopped and listened. Only the deceiving sound of crickets filled the evening air and he paid them little heed. After a time he sat down on a fallen tree, drew up his knees for a table, and began to write.

Dear Annette,

Oh, dear wife if only you were here to see what I see! As I wrote to you two days ago, we came upon a great wooded hill with a breathtaking waterfall. I have spent the last two days exploring the area's fine forests with my officers, Denis and Pascal. Do not worry – the British military do not have any numbers here and we avoid most contact of any kind.

As we made our way to the top of its flattened plateau, our eyes came upon an enchanted scene that you would never believe. Yet I must share it with my quill as clearly as I can. Dearest Annette, there is a lake on the top of the mountain! It is quite small compared to the great lakes that I have seen but it is oh-so-flawless in its beauty.

I have learned that the Mohawk Indians here call it Onokenoga, or Lake of the Gods. For them, it is a sacred place where spirits dwell. Each spring, they offer gifts to the spirits who reside there to ensure a successful crop in the coming year.

Others tell me the little lake is bottomless or has subterranean passages. I can tell you it does not appear to have any water source itself, even though it sends its white falls plunging over the side of this great hill.

I grow weary of the war, Annette. This unspoiled land gives me new resolve to bring you here with me. After the war, we can start anew here together, above or below this small mountain with its silent lake. We can build a whole new life! I know you have wanted to leave Paris for the countryside; here, there is countryside for everyone. We could be happy.

In my imagination, I can see how quaint farm houses might soon dot this land. I can see rich grain fields, thick apple orchards and field after field of sweet-smelling clover. There are distant, rolling hills and forests bursting with oak, maple and hickory trees.

I am going to ease my way over the great hill now to see this wonder again while my officers return to the ship. I haven't much more time but I wanted a chance to think alone. I think of you often,

Yours Always,

Joseph

Chapter 18

Exodus

By the following day the word had spread. From on top of an outcropping of land over the bay, John, Moll and Lou watched the sun-lit waterway with open mouths. The bay was speckled with boat after boat of people who were on their way out of Stone Mills. The colonel had not yet ordered an evacuation, but many were choosing to leave anyway – especially those who lived on top of the mountain.

They could see Solomon Brook talking with people and it was obvious to John that they were begging him to let them buy the boats he had been working on for other customers, even those that were barely finished.

On land, John could see the Carnahan family wagon moving through the village and making its way to the harsh Danforth Road.

"Look," said Moll, pointing. "There's the Rutter's, too." John looked and saw George and Abaline Rutter, farmers from on top of the mountain. In front of Pringle's General Store they were loading several supplies onto their wagon. That could only mean a long journey was ahead. They had just moved here last year from Bloomfield.

John knew the people had simply had enough. Lake creatures, missing farmers, a bloody shirt in the lake, and now there was a missing police constable who had tried to investigate. The busiest man on the lake was the ferryman, Jacob Adams, who had been taking people across the short reach to Adolphustown last night and all morning.

"John, who is that?" asked Moll. From the south, a chestnut-coloured horse carrying a man clad in a black suit trotted into the village. A small gathering of dust encircled the horse's hooves as it entered Stone Mills.

"It's Pastor Macdowell," said John, squinting. "What's he doing here?"

Stone Mills didn't yet have its own church. Most folks who were Presbyterian made the trip to Hallowell, the largest town in the area, at least monthly if not more regularly. They wanted to hear the pastor's sermons. Hallowell also attracted people from Bloomfield, Waupoos and other small villages.

But with everything going on this week, he wondered how many people had actually left for church this Sunday morning. John, Moll and Lou moved toward the centre of the village where the horse and rider had stopped. Already, a small group had gathered.

"People of Stone Mills!" he hollered. "I understand this is a time of fear…a time of worry. I could see by your slight numbers at service today that I should bring the word of the Lord to you this afternoon. If you are so inclined, please join me at the clearing," he gestured.

John whirled toward Moll and Lou. "Let's get out of here before Mother sees the pastor and decides …"

"John Macdonald! Moll and Louisa!" yelled Helen, beckoning all three.

Too late.

They sighed in unison. John, Moll and Louisa dragged their feet toward the grassy clearing where the pastor was directing. Their mother and father had already wandered over and nodded to the area where they should sit. John wished George didn't have family obligations for most of the day; he could have at least sat with his friend. Then again, George was Catholic and his family may not have wanted him to attend a Presbyterian service.

Pastor Macdowell was a veteran preacher. Having come to the area at the invitation of Peter Van Alstine, the original owner of the mills in the village, he was at home here. He walked about, coaxing and persuading people to join him, undaunted by the bay full of boats and the obvious feeling of anxiety in the village.

He identified four, young men who could act as messengers to knock on doors throughout the village to let them know the pastor was in town for service. Two would work the lower part of the village; the other two would scale the mountain and let the people there know.

Twenty minutes later, he had a small crowd before him, spread out over the clearing in roughly-created rows. Of the people who did choose to attend, John spotted the young boy he had knocked over last week. The boy who looked like James.

The young lad was sitting with what might have been his whole family, including his mother, father, grandfather and a younger sister. The boy kept staring at John so he waved and smiled. He looked away with spooked eyes. John realized the young boy was likely still afraid of him after getting flattened by a flour-covered, shrieking figure.

John tried to focus on the pastor's words but he had too much on his mind. Instead, he watched those who had come, reading the worry in their faces, including his own family's. They were fixated on Pastor Macdowell, leaning on his every word, hoping the clue to their anxiety was right there in his sentences.

"John," whispered Lou.

"What?"

"I don't want to leave."

John looked back at the boats in the bay. "Me either, Lou."

She bumped him again. "Someone needs to find out what that thing is that we saw – do you think it could be a big fish?"

"Sure – sure it could be," John said, trying to sound convincing. But John didn't believe himself as soon as the words left his mouth. "Someone will figure it out, Lou, don't you worry."

Lou nodded and turned toward the pastor. Everyone acted polite and composed. But the pastor's words didn't resonate with John. It wasn't that John was a disbeliever. Everyone in good society was a believer and that was the way things worked.

But John wondered if he should be sitting back and waiting for God – or anyone else – to figure out what was going on in Stone Mills. He was worried God might not have the same timeline as he did. At the rate the village was shrinking, who knows how long his father would last before he'd see it as a reason to move on? Not to mention he had to go back to Kingston within only days. That might not matter so much to God but it sure mattered to John. But what could he do?

As he glanced around, John realized his uncle was nowhere to be seen. "Where's the colonel?" he asked his mother.

"I wouldn't know," said his mother. "He left late last night and said he'd return soon. Now pay attention."

Her eyes turned toward the pastor. John faced the

front where the pastor was speaking but he couldn't stop wondering where his uncle had gone. He hoped he wouldn't just vanish, like Mr. Rightmyer and Constable Ogden. John looked around more. Big Solomon Brook was spread out on the grass, along with his wife, Rachel. So were Hannah Pringle and Darius Marshall, who sat together. John wondered if Mr. Marshall was courting Hannah.

John could see Constable Ogden's wife, sitting with a friend, dabbing at her eyes as the pastor spoke. Darius and Hannah, who were sitting nearby, comforted her. He couldn't imagine what was going through Mrs. Ogden's mind, with her husband never returning from the lake. If it were anyone else and not the constable, John knew most would assume he was off drinking at a tavern. But not Constable Ogden. He didn't drink and everyone knew he was as dependable as an ox.

Even though he had been tuning out, John noticed Pastor Macdowell was avoiding direct references to the serpent of Lake on the Mountain. Moll leaned over and whispered, "Have you noticed Mr. Pitman isn't here?"

John's eyes widened. Moll was right. Nathaniel Pitman didn't have many friends, but he almost always made the trip to Hallowell to hear Pastor Macdowell's sermons. At the real church, the saw mill operator usually sat in the back row, alone. When the service ended, he left first without talking to anyone.

Helen reached behind Moll to tap John on the shoulder. "Remember, once service is over, you're not to go to the lake – whether George is able to come over today or not."

John nodded solemnly. "Yes, Mother. George and I have no plans to go to the lake."

After what seemed like an insufferable long time, Pastor Macdowell closed his sermon with parting words about keeping faith in the hour of greatest need. As people began to file away, the Boggart family shuffled past. Owen looked at John but didn't try to run into his shoulder as he usually did, not with adults around.

Hugh found a group of men and began chatting. Even in times of stress John knew his father liked to socialize a great deal. At one point the men broke out into nervous laughter about something, no doubt trying to lighten the heavy mood. John saw his mother sigh. He knew she was worried about his father's focus lately.

John needed to think things through. He wondered if George was going to be able to make it here today, or if his parents would keep him home. Maybe they didn't like the rumours from the village either.

Many adults spoke with the pastor after his sermon and thanked him for coming. When John sensed it was an appropriate time, he approached.

"Pastor Macdowell?"

"Yes, young John Macdonald, how have you been?

Growing like a weed you are. Good to see you here today." He put an arm around his shoulder for a moment and smiled. "It's a good last-minute turnout – although I don't see Nathaniel. That's a surprise."

"That's what I thought," said John. "I always see him at your church in Hallowell – not many would guess he's such a man of faith."

The pastor nodded and rubbed the back of his head. "Well, when you've suffered like that man has, that can change you."

"Suffered...how?"

Pastor Macdowell lowered his voice and John leaned in. "Quite a few years ago he ran a saw mill in Niagara. A little girl was killed when she and a friend sneaked into the mill."

John swallowed. "How did she...?"

"Die?" finished the pastor. "While they were playing she slipped off a ledge and ended up dead on the blades below."

"I didn't know..." said John.

"Sure, he wouldn't talk much about it. But he took it hard. Doesn't want kids anywhere near his mill – and who can blame him, really?"

John made a mental note to tell George.

"Pastor Macdowell, I was just wondering – how come you didn't mention what's going on up on the mountain. About the creature everyone's seeing?"

The pastor sighed and led John a little further away from the crowd. "I don't want to encourage the stories, son. You see, I don't believe much in serpents and creatures that can't be explained. That's not to say I don't believe that there are some fantastic things, some wondrous things in our world. But that's not quite the same as a belief in sea serpents."

"Well, does the bible mention sea creatures, Pastor Macdowell?" John asked.

The older man thought about it, stroking his greying whiskers. "Well, there is Isaiah 27:1 which references a great leviathan in the sea." He cleared his throat. "Here's the gist of it."

"...the Lord, with his...great and strong sword shall punish the leviathan...and he shall slay the dragon that is in the sea."

John raised his eyebrows. "Wow, a real leviathan?"

Pastor Macdowell smiled. "I'm not so sure that Isaiah meant an actual leviathan. I've always found that a person's fear might be the greatest monster to overcome, John. Listen, it was good to see you again."

John nodded and the pastor moved on to speak with others. He could feel the people moving around him, talking and visiting. But John no longer saw anyone. In his mind he only saw what the Mohawk called the Lake of the Gods. He wondered if he could survive against a leviathan. He wondered if he had the courage to try.

Chapter 19

Manifest Destiny

"John?"

"What, Lou?" John dug hard into the ground with his shovel to get the deepest potatoes. Lou knocked the dirt from them and gathered them in a basket as he continued to dig.

"Do you think Pastor Macdowell made everyone feel better today?" she asked. Moll, holding an apron full of green beans, exchanged glances with John.

Twilight cast a wide, purpled layer over the hushed village. There was no sign of the small crowd that had listened to the pastor earlier in the afternoon. Like her younger sister, Moll, too, wondered if most people had left the church service feeling better off. Although at first soothed by the pastor's words, Moll felt her previous anxieties returning.

"I don't know Lou...maybe some," said John. "How about you – do you feel any better?"

She shook her head. "No – I don't like that serpent

and if Father says we have to move, I won't go," she said, taking the time to cross her arms.

"Lou, I know how you feel but don't worry about that right now. Listen, your basket's pretty much full anyway – why don't you just go on in. Moll and I will be in after we finish this last row."

"Hmmph." Lou picked up the basket and a potato rolled out. She kicked it into a bush with the ball of her foot.

"Lou!" said Moll. "You stop that." Lou disappeared around to the front of the house with her basket of potatoes.

"She's impossible," said Moll. She felt her cheeks turn pink at her sister's behaviour. Moll always felt personally responsible for Lou's actions. Maybe that was part of being the eldest sister.

John shook his head and grinned, but Moll watched his face quickly turn reflective again as he worked the shovel. The two worked in silence for the next fifteen minutes, listening to the thick white thread of falling water, pounding the water wheel behind the mill. After she brushed more dirt from the pile of potatoes that John was creating beside them, Moll sneaked a long glance at her brother. He was acting oddly lately. Was he planning something?

"What's bothering you?" she asked.

"Who – me?" asked John. He refocused on the last

hill of potatoes and sliced the ground with the shovel. "Nothing."

"Where do you think the colonel went?" Moll asked. "It was odd not having him there at supper for the first time all week."

John shrugged and slapped at a mosquito. "Who knows – he's been acting aloof since he got here."

Moll wondered if this was what was upsetting her brother. He and the colonel were very close with all the time John spent in Kingston. But no, it wasn't that. The way he was looking around all the time there was something else going on.

"Are you planning on going somewhere?" she asked. He shot her a defiant look. Then she knew.

"John, don't you go up there, it's not safe."

"You didn't say it was a bad idea before."

"That was during the day – it's evening now and you'd be alone!" She held his stare but felt the weight of the decision he had made.

Just then a man Moll recognized as a farmer from atop the mountain came into the village with his horse and wagon team. His drove them at a full trot and headed straight toward John and Moll.

***

Darius Marshall knew that it took a visionary to be

able to see what he could see. He pictured the ships that would unload hundreds of American soldiers, staged in intervals. They would fortify themselves and then launch destabilizing sneak attacks, both at York and at Kingston.

Of course it would take ongoing troops. But what better place for them to land than in an unexpected rural area, with an endless connection of waterways to key ports? From such a vantage point, Kingston and York would fall in no time.

He pictured Edgar, soft and corrupt, pleading for mercy from his home in York. He tried to think of what might happen to Sophia during such an encounter. Would he spare her life?

Darius absently looked toward the back of the room where Anson Rightmyer and Constable Ogden sat, slumped in their chairs, gagged and bound. The grinning farmer noted that both had once again exhausted themselves with their futile struggling. He was enjoying the quiet as he rubbed the frail sparrow beneath his thumb. The bird extended its wings and made a soft, chirping noise.

"Not yet, not yet." Darius folded the bird's wings gently to its side. "I know you're restless. Shhh."

It was all happening more quickly than he would have ever imagined. But truly, there was no better time. Darius was certain of former President Madison's belief in the destiny of the United States of America. Surely President Adams felt the same way? The notion that the U.S. was destined to one day rule over the entire North American continent seemed logical. Unquestionable.

A shadow glided into the cabin and spoke. "I just sent out the word. A schooner flying the British flag has left the area, on its way to Oswego in the U.S. When it gets halfway across it will raise the American flag. How many ships will follow it back?"

"Another schooner will," said Darius.

"That's all? We need more."

Darius waved him off. "It's enough for now to secure the area. I'm sure more will follow once President Adams learns of our plans to liberate this colony."

The shadow hesitated. "What do you mean, 'learns?' You told us the president already knows."

"Yes," said Darius soothingly. "Of course – that's exactly what I meant." Another shadow eased into the cabin.

"What is it?" asked Darius. He set the bird on the table and tucked it in with a soft cloth.

"There's a child up here – one of the Macdonald girls. Do you want me to deal with this?" the voice said.

Darius shook his head. "I'll handle her. Give her something to remember."

Chapter 20

'That Lake's No Good'

The farmer and his horses slowed in front of John and Moll.

"Hi, Mr. Purdy," said John. "Are you leaving, too?"

"That's right – had more than enough of this place, I have. Got a brother east of York who says there's good land there, too. I'll take him up on that idea, I will."

"Alright, good luck," said John. He wasn't sure why the man had stopped.

"I just thought I'd mention," said the farmer, "on account of you might not knowing."

"What's that?" asked John.

"I recognized your little sister up there. Saw her headed towards the lake just as I was heading down the mountain road. Thought you might want to know. That lake's no good, you know."

"Lou?" said Moll, putting a hand to her mouth. "Oh my God! She must have never gone back inside! But why would she go up there?"

"The lake's no good at all," repeated the farmer, who began to turn his wagon around for the road. "You'll take care of it, then?"

"Yes, Mr. Purdy, thank you for stopping," said Moll. She turned back to John, but her brother had vanished.

**

John climbed. The knot in his stomach grew tighter as he thought about Lou. He was afraid, before, when he thought about what he had seen in the lake. He was terrified now, to think that his little sister had gone there alone this evening.

He should have realized, when she was asking him questions about Pastor Macdowell's service, that she was going to try something stupid. She didn't want to move away either and was going to try and figure out what was in the lake. John knew Lou was feisty and strong. Determined. But she was only nine, thought John. He climbed faster.

He leaned into the great hill and scaled it, using the trees and firm roots to give him extra traction. Halfway up he looked back at the bay and the village below. It was quieter now. Even in the twilight, he could still see bateaux on the waters of the bay. The fear had spread like a great wave that threatened everything in its wake.

He glanced at the looming saw mill to his left and

avoided its dark gaze, turning right until he reached the plateau where the mountain flattened. As he scrabbled over, John carefully looked around. A strong wind blew in from the north and whipped John's locks of hair.

Then he caught sight of Lou out on the lake, riding one of Nathaniel Pitman's battered, wooden rafts. The saw mill operator had a few of them leaning against the mill to move wood. He ran to get his own raft into the water.

The overcast sky had conspired with twilight leaving the sky paralyzed in grey. A great wind swarmed the lakeside as John bent down and shoved the flat, wooden square toward the lake, grabbing a thick oar at the same time. The scent of a dead fish caught in his nostrils as he struggled with the raft.

"Lou!" he called out just loud enough for her to hear. He didn't want them to be heard on the lake and nor did he want anything living in the lake to come at them. All he knew was that he had to help Lou.

Lou turned her head and frowned. "Go away, John. I'm going to find that fish thing. I don't want to leave here either, you know."

"Lou – get back here!" John said. He waded up to his calves and gave a final look at the saw mill to make sure no one had seen. John then leapt aboard and pushed off. With the help of the wooden oar and an urgent wind, he pushed off toward the middle of Lake on the Mountain.

Chapter 21

The Leviathan

Moll hurried and gathered the rest of the vegetables into the bushel basket.

"Moll, John, Lou!" shouted Helen from the doorway. "Are you waiting for more vegetables to grow?"

"Coming!" Moll shouted back, even though she was the only one left. Moll heard the door shut again and took a deep breath, wondering what to do. Just then, she saw George sprinting down the main path into the village.

"Moll, where is John?" he asked.

She held her hand to her lips and motioned him over to the garden, behind the Macdonald house. "He just went up there," she said. She pointed to the dark, forested mountain.

"What? To the lake – by himself? Mon dieu, why would he –"

"Because we found out Lou went up to the lake alone. Mother and Father don't even know yet and

Mother's just called us in! What are you doing here?"

"I was not allowed to come over earlier – too much work to do. Mother asked me to borrow some tea for her. It has darkened quickly," said George, looking around.

A strong wind whipped Moll's bronze-coloured hair into her face. She looked up at the great hill. "I'm going up there, too," she said to herself, as much as to George.

"I will go with you," George said.

Moll glanced over her shoulder to ensure they were not seen running behind the house toward the forested mountain. She did not notice a handful of long, lean boats in the Bay of Quinte, as they eased onto the shore.

***

John steadied himself in the centre of the raft, using the oar for balance. He dropped to his knees once he got farther out, dipping the oar from side to side to gain momentum.

"I'm coming, Lou." It was obvious she was having trouble with the weight of the oar she was using. It looked like it might pull her overboard, if she wasn't careful. The strong wind and her growing fears had forced her onto her knees as well.

John remembered the time Cornelius had let him control the bateau on the bay. It took balance and skill and that was a larger vessel. John had never done anything like this with winds this strong, though, or on a small raft. He didn't know what to expect as he rowed out.

Focusing his eyes into the middle of the dark lake, John studied its surface. He watched the wind draw long, trembling lines onto the surface of the water. He clenched his stomach. But there was no sign of anything else. There was no sign of the leviathan.

He closed in on Lou who was still struggling with her oar in the wind. As she turned, her dark hair blew back and John could see her anxious face.

"John? I don't think I can do this," Lou said. "It's so windy." She turned carefully on her knees on top of her raft to face John who was now only fifteen feet away.

"That's okay, Lou. Easy now on that thing. You're doing great. Listen, I'm going to try to pull up close and…"

"John!"

John turned his head toward the shore at the sound of his name and nearly lost his balance. "Moll? George?" he yelled over the wind.

"What are you doing?" screamed Moll. "Get off the lake!" They were running around the perimeter of the lake, trying to get closer.

"That's what we're trying to –" John began.

"Oh, no!" George yelled. "Behind you – near Lou!"

The sound of breaking water caught John's ear. He looked deeper into the centre of the lake and his heart raced. Cresting the surface of the lake, the same serpent-like, green neck and head they had seen before near the old tree appeared directly in front of Lou's raft. The serpent advanced.

Lou screamed. She fell onto her back on the raft, holding her arms up instinctively. The creature, dark green and distorted in twilight, continued to move silently toward her.

John looked at his little sister on the raft and thought of James as he paddled hard toward her. Maybe it hadn't been directly his fault, but he had failed his little brother. He wouldn't fail his sister, too. John pointed his raft straight toward the creature.

"Hey! Ugly!" John yelled. The creature paused in the water as if aware of a second person out on the lake for the first time. It slowly turned its head. John's momentum was carrying his raft straight toward the creature.

He moved from his knees to his feet. Hunched, at first, he tightened his grip on the long, thick oar. John could see the creature's head and neck move ever closer. He heard Moll scream again from the shore.

"Come on," said John under his breath. "Just a little closer."

John bent his knees and gripped the oar as tightly as

he could. As his raft floated close enough to reach the serpent, John swung. He aimed at the creature's neck and twisted the oar at the last second to ensure the narrow, sharper side would strike.

With a dull series of cracks the creature's neck crumpled in half. Segments of dark, green cloth separated and floated on the water. Now uncovered, John could see long, bent branches tied together, many broken where the oar had struck.

Before he could register surprise, John could hear furious splashing underneath the parts of the creature, including two light-weight, floating humps which rose to the surface, bobbing sideways.

John saw the back of a man begin to swim toward the shoreline but then lost sight of him as he ducked under the water's surface. After helping Lou onto his raft, he turned toward the direction that the man was swimming. But the extra weight of Lou and the wind pushing against him made it difficult to move quickly.

When he finally began to move the raft toward shore, he realized the swimmer was heading straight for George.

And now, Moll was nowhere in sight.

Chapter 22

Battles Are Won in the Mind

"George! Run!" said John. He wondered where Moll had gone.

Home, I hope.

The man was an exceptionally fast swimmer. As he emerged from the water, John could see, even in the fading light, that it was Darius Marshall. Clad only in a thin, green, short-sleeved shirt and shorts, he rushed toward George even before he was out of the water. George pivoted away and ran along the beach toward the edge of the mountain. But within seconds, Darius closed the gap and reached out to grab him. His hand closed on George's shirt.

But not for long. From the direction of the saw mill an immense, bearded man rushed toward Darius and seized him in a bear hug.

"It's Mr. Pitman!" John said to Lou as they reached the shoreline in the raft. Darius struggled but the saw mill operator was too powerful. John and Lou could see their older sister running from the saw mill toward them. Obviously Moll had gone to get help, John realized.

John, George, Moll and Lou turned their attention on the still-struggling Darius Marshall. Nathaniel shoved him to the ground and held him using one knee and both of his tree-trunk-sized arms.

"Go get your father and any other men you can find," he growled.

John nodded but before he could act he heard a series of clicks in the gathering dark.

"Don't move, boy."

The voice was cold. Authoritative. John froze as he saw a long gun pointed at him. "You," the same man said to Nathaniel. "Get off him – now." He pointed the gun at the saw mill operator.

Other men emerged from the shadows of the forest, rifles aimed at Nathaniel Pitman and John, Moll and George. They wore knives strapped to their belts and were dressed in green and brown. John counted eight more men besides Darius Marshall. Judging by the way they moved, John was certain they were soldiers.

The burly saw mill operator rose to his feet and released Darius, who leaped from the ground and wiped his brow with his forearm. He laughed and rubbed his thinning, wet hair with his hands. His face was now dirty but his smile was as wide as John had ever seen.

Blood began to spill out of his mouth where he had been hurt in the scuffle. He spit on the ground in front of Nathaniel Pitman.

"What a grip, yes siree," he said. He glared through his twitching smile. John was still trying to make sense of everything that was happening.

"Why did you do it?" asked John. "Why did you create that…thing out there?" John glanced at the darkened lake. "And who are they?"

Darius smirked. "They're soldiers of the United States of America." The soldiers stood stiffly with their backs to the edge of the mountain.

"And even they didn't think it would work," Darius said. "Look around, John. Battles are won in the mind, aren't they?" He tapped his head. "I have to say, for a Brit I was surprised you would challenge like that. Out in the middle of a supposedly haunted, dark lake." He sighed and wrung the water out of the front of his shirt. "I think you've gone and wrecked my little creature's neck."

John realized Darius sounded different now – he had an accent he didn't recognize. "I thought you were a friend," said John.

"Changed my mind. Is that allowed in your Upper Canada, son? Or does the Family Compact control that too? You see, once you started talking politics with me, I knew you were like all the rest."

"The Tories – or anyone else – didn't make you frighten everyone away from Stone Mills," said Moll.

"And no one is making you point guns at us – except you," said George.

Darius began to pace in front of them, keeping his distance from Nathaniel Pitman, even though there were eight men pointing guns to protect him. "What you people don't understand is that it takes sacrifice to build a democracy. It takes courage," he said.

Hearing no reply he pounded his open palm. "It takes sweat and dedication," he shouted.

"And it takes a coward to point guns at children," said Nathaniel. John wondered if the saw mill operator would end up getting them all killed.

"I don't go out of my way to harm people," said Darius. His grin was lopsided now. "But when stumbling neighbours and prying, law enforcement types come calling, then it leaves a man no choice."

John swallowed. "You're the one…you killed Mr. Rightmyer and Constable Ogden!"

Darius sighed. "Did I? Oh, it's possible, son. Interfering, they were. Very nosy. My cabin was set up as my base, you see. That's not for outsiders to poke around at, especially Brits."

Darius spun around and faced one of the men working for him. "How many people are left in this pathetic village?"

"Very few. At last check even the British colonel seems to have left. From what we've seen, the only ones remaining are the Macdonald's..."

John, Moll and Lou all looked at one another.

"...the shipbuilder, Solomon Brook. Him," the soldier said, nodding to Nathaniel. "The general store owner. And there's a handful of farmers left on the perimeter."

"Hannah," Darius said. He sounded less hostile than he had a moment ago. "Now there's a woman who would understand all of this."

He paused as if deep in thought. In the encroaching shadows, John thought he saw calm on Darius' face and wondered if he was having a change of heart. He motioned all of the soldiers to gather around him, except for one. The lone, American soldier kept his gun pointed at Nathaniel who stood only a few feet away.

John strained to hear as the other seven soldiers leaned on their rifles and listened to Darius.

"Round up all of the villagers, except Hannah," Darius said. "Tonight we rid ourselves of those who stand in the way of freedom."

The men nodded. "I didn't think this would work," said one. Darius placed his hand on his shoulder. "We're going to show the Brits how to run a country, if it's the last thing..."

Before Darius could finish, men with long guns

swarmed over the ridge of the mountain. They raised their rifles at the American soldiers. John felt a surge of excitement.

A platoon of British soldiers!

"Put down your weapons!" yelled one. "Now!" ordered another. The last man to appear, wearing his signature red coat, was Lieutenant Colonel Macpherson. The American soldiers realized they were outnumbered and outflanked by the British soldiers. All of the U.S. soldiers except for the one guarding Nathaniel, John, Moll and Lou quickly surrendered their weapons.

"Colonel Macpherson!" John beamed.

Before one of the colonel's soldiers could take action on the remaining U.S. soldier, the armed American swung his rifle toward the line of British infantrymen.

Chapter 23

Of Monsters and Men

Before the American gunman's rifle could go off, a British soldier aimed and fired. The American grabbed the top of his shoulder where he had been grazed and fell to his knees. He looked up with a snarl and reached for his fallen weapon. Before he could pick it up, the massive boot of Nathaniel Pitman crushed his hand.

"Ahhhh!" The soldier's scream was louder than when the bullet had hit him. Nathaniel reached down, snatched the rifle up, and handed it to the colonel.

Darius, strands of dark hair hanging about one side of his face, smiled in fierce spasms. "You're too late, old man." He turned to the colonel and grinned through blood-stained teeth.

"The word has already gone out. Soon this ghost village will be overrun by American soldiers." He laughed and spit a wad of blood in front of the colonel's feet.

The retired officer moved his moustache with his lips

and stared down at Darius without flinching. "I assume you're referring to the schooner you had waiting off Waupoos Island, on its way to Oswego?" John watched Darius' face fall.

"It was intercepted about thirty miles from shore by a British sloop. Its small crew was taken prisoner. Just like you will be."

Darius wilted further and fell silent. The colonel made sure John, Moll, Lou and George were safe and thanked Nathaniel for his intervention. He explained that their parents were staying at home until the area was secured. John told his uncle about the lake creature and how it had been an artificial creation of Darius Marshall's to scare people away.

"But what I don't understand is why would someone from here want to scare people away so American soldiers could attack?"

"He's not from here," said the colonel. "He's an American citizen – from Kentucky – a decorated ex-soldier who fought for the U.S. in the War of 1812. But he's been on the run from the U.S. army ever since he shot and killed four British soldiers long after the Treaty of Ghent was signed. He never let go of the war and wasn't following orders – not the mark of a good soldier, to say the least. But we knew he might still command loyalty of some of the men from his unit."

"You told us we were working for President Adams!"

said one of the American soldiers. "On a covert mission," he added, straining against the arms of the two British soldiers who held him.

The colonel scoffed. "President Adams wouldn't know him unless he was looking at a list of vigilantes."

Darius flipped his thinning, brown hair back that hung in front of his eyes. "My country lost sight of what was important. When President Madison was in power, during the war, he would have understood."

The colonel wiped his brow and as John watched him he wondered how difficult this mission had been for his aging uncle to endure. "How did you know who he really was?" asked John.

"We didn't have a description so it took me awhile to piece it together," said his uncle. "It was a lot of discussions with neighbours. But once I learned the backgrounds of people here and stacked it up with pieces I learned from the U.S. government, it began to add up. The lake serpent threw me off. But learning from the U.S. that he was a renowned strategist and considered unorthodox in his battle methods… well, I wondered if they were connected."

Darius spoke. "This whole continent should have been American by now. Only the British could have created this place in their arrogant, insufferable way."

John watched his uncle give a lopsided grin. "You can pretend it's all politics," said the colonel, "but a lot of this was personal, too. Meaning your wife, of course."

Darius raised his head. "We came here to make a new life," he said in a whisper.

Moll looked at the colonel, confused. "Both of them came to Upper Canada?"

Her uncle nodded. "He and his wife, Sophia, learned to hide their accents well. They adapted – had to, since they fled to York once the U.S. Army came after him."

Darius spoke to the ground. "Only six months here and Sophia was already being taken from me by the Family Compact. By Edgar." He looked up. "Do you see? The Tories took that away. They took Sophia away from me."

"You can't blame your failed marriage on the Tories," said the colonel.

"And then I realized," said Darius, "that the Family Compact took everything away from everyone. I realized it wasn't about me. That I had to set the people here free."

"I find it interesting that a man headed to prison is making a speech about freedom," said the colonel.

Darius' etched smile faded some as he studied his feet. Then he looked at the colonel. "Reformers are not alone, old man. There are people – like Mackenzie – who will carry on. You'll see – change is coming."

"Why does change have to happen all at once?"

asked John. "Just because I'm a British subject – and I'll die a British subject some day – doesn't mean we can't grow. Not everything happens overnight."

Darius shook his head. "I did the right thing."

"If you really want to do the right thing, you'll tell them where Mr. Rightmyer and Constable Ogden are," said John.

A soft, female voice rose from the edge of the lake. "Darius?"

Everyone turned and saw the slender outline of Hannah Pringle. The moon had risen above the tree line, cutting shards of light across her anxious face. "You're responsible for all of this?"

"Hannah…" the ex-soldier began. His eyes softened as hers hardened.

"I believed in you…believed in what you stood for," she said. "But I didn't know you were capable of this." She dabbed at her eyes with a white cloth.

"Did you believe in him enough to create *The Stone Mills Reformer*?" asked Moll. All eyes turned to Moll. "I saw her the other day with ink on her neck. I wasn't sure that it was ink at the time. Then later I realized she was likely the only one in the village, other than farmers, who had the space to hold a printing press," she said, referring to her large, back shed.

Hannah gave a shrug and a weak smile. "That old printing press...I figured it would be a good way to help along the reform effort. Reformers aren't popular though now, are they? Thought I'd best keep that to myself. When you startled me that day out back," she said to Moll, "I wondered if you'd figure it out."

"It was you?" asked Darius. "You mean you did that for me?"

Hannah didn't answer. Instead she turned and watched the small, lapping lake a few feet to her right. At the edge of the water, the broken creature's neck washed ashore at her feet.

"I suppose I did do it for you. Of course, I didn't know you were a monster – did I?"

***

The next morning word travelled like it always does. From family to family, friend to friend, business to business and every other possible combination of folks passing on the news. Stone Mills was back to normal, according to the official and unofficial word.

Anson Rightmyer and Constable Ogden were rescued from Darius Marshall's hidden cabin, shaken but alive. Lieutenant Colonel Macpherson had gone back to Kingston the same night, with all the British soldiers and his nine, American prisoners in tow. Before he left he had quickly dropped off an injured sparrow they had found inside the cabin for Moll and Lou to look after.

Many people had approached John, George, Moll and Lou to thank them, congratulate them and to get them to retell the entire story. John was usually the one who took over at this part. It was George's observation that John's serpent in the story kept getting larger with every retelling, but few seemed to notice or mind.

Around the supper table that night, the talk was still about the events of the previous evening. But there was something John still didn't understand. "So the colonel didn't come because of the news sheet at all?" he asked his mother and father.

Helen shook her head while she sliced a loaf of bread. "I guess that was only an interesting coincidence. Who knew it could be Hannah Pringle involved in that?"

"Even though Donald's retired I have to admit he knows this area well," said Hugh. "I wondered how the other British soldiers got here. Turns out he spoke to the Kingston garrison commander who agreed to dispatch soldiers to the area to respond to any conflict if the colonel required. They were close enough to get here in time, but not so close to alert suspicion."

"And Darius Marshall wasn't even his real name?" asked Moll. "That's what the colonel said when we left the top of the mountain last night."

"Sure, he would have dropped his real name in order to hide out for as long as he did," said Hugh. "Who knows what his real name is? Doesn't matter much now – he'll either be in jail for life or more likely be hanged back in the U.S." John swallowed and exchanged glances with Moll and Lou.

By the time the day was over, John felt happy to crawl into his bed and blow out his oil lamp. He pulled his sheet up to his neck just as he heard a light rap at his door. "Come in," said John.

His mother stood in his bedroom doorway holding one of the lit candles she and Moll often made together. Her great shadow behind her flickered and filled his room. "That was a courageous thing you did, going after your sister," said Helen. "I know I wasn't happy at first, with you taking off like that. But it was a brave thing."

"Lou was the brave one," said John. "She wanted to see for herself, whether or not there was a creature in the lake." He paused. "I just didn't want…"

"You didn't want what?" Helen urged.

"I didn't want to lose her in such a terrible way. Like James," said John.

John watched his mother's eyes well up. She reached out with her free hand and steadied the one that held the lit candle.

"One day…well, you just mark my words, John Macdonald. You'll make more than an ordinary man."

Chapter 24

A Matter of Perspective

John couldn't believe it had only been three days since the man known as Darius Marshall was arrested and jailed in Kingston awaiting his trial. Stone Mills had returned to life. For three, straight days, there was a steady trickle of families moving back into the village, below and above the mountain, ready to start again.

He knew Hannah Pringle was devastated about the outcome. His mother had gone to the store more often than she needed to check up on her. While most people were displeased that she had supported the cause of reform, Helen had told her son she ran the only general store in town and would survive the extra scrutiny.

John and George exited the flour mill where they had been working and turned toward the forested mountain. They had helped Hugh Macdonald all morning at the mill and John had successfully negotiated some time off to spend with George. After all, in two days he would be headed back to Kingston with Cornelius for the fall and long winter.

Before they could disappear into the woods, John heard his name being called. He turned to see Anson Rightmyer and Constable Charles Ogden making their way toward them from the centre of the village. It was the first time John had seen them since he was told they had been found safe in the American vigilante's cabin.

"John Macdonald, I hope Anson and I aren't keeping you from something important," said the constable. The top of his bald head was wet with perspiration as he ambled over. Anson Rightmyer looked skinnier than usual, but wore a content smile.

"Not at all, it's really great to see you both," said John. Everyone shook hands and John felt his eyes drawn to the slim, farmer's hand with the missing finger. John mentally kicked himself for sneaking a look.

"We can't thank you enough for what you did up by the lake. Anson, here, he got the worst of those soldiers," said Constable Ogden. "Of course, he was there longer, too."

The lanky farmer looked at the ground and shrugged. "It wasn't something I'd wish on anyone, that's for sure," said Anson. "But we're both sure grateful for the way you and George – well, the whole Macdonald family, helped us out. Especially your uncle, of course."

Constable Ogden wiped his head with his palm.

"When we saw those British soldiers enter the cabin, after all those days stuck in there…it's hard to describe how good that felt. I'll go back to finding stray horses any day of the week after that much excitement."

John and George laughed. They said their goodbyes and both men moved on toward the mill and John guessed they were going to see his father. Knowing his father, John figured they might be awhile as every detail was talked about.

They made their way into the forest behind the mill and John pulled out the treasure map. The two discussed possibilities, chatting excitedly. John led the way for twenty minutes as they walked around the forest. But nothing seemed to match the map's lines.

"This way," said George, pointing to a spot on the map and then at a large oak tree. "Could that tree be this line here?" he asked, pointing to the map.

John sighed and let George lead him to the oak tree. He looked around, looked at the map again, and then finally turned around and slumped against the oak. George joined him, letting his back slide down. The mid-day, August sun perforated the tree's branches, creating laces of light on their arms.

"I don't think this tree is the place, George. But I just can't shake the feeling that the treasure is near here somewhere. The French admiral, who Jeremiah Thacker said he saw as a kid, was just down there along the water's edge," John said. He imagined the dying admiral on the shoreline and tried to picture Mr. Thacker as a boy not much older than himself.

"Oui, but that does not mean the treasure was near here. Maybe the admiral just got back from somewhere else and that is where he happened to collapse," said George.

"Maybe. I just have a sense it's nearby, otherwise he would have given him another clue as to where to start looking.

"Unless he could not say it because he was dying."

John sighed again. "It would help if I hadn't soaked this map when I fell into the lake," said John, disgusted. He tossed the map to the ground a few feet away and rubbed his eyes. When his vision cleared he stared at the upside down map. "No…could it be?" Like a sling-shot John left the sturdy oak and picked up the map, holding it upside down as he had just viewed it.

"What?" asked George.

"Look at this. We keep thinking these lines coming down right here," he said, pointing, "was the way he hastily drew trees. What if these aren't trees at all. What if this is a waterfall?"

John felt a surge of excitement. Between the new perspective he was taking as he looked at the map, and the slightly smeared lines, it gave everything a fresh look.

George frowned. "You mean the waterfall behind the

flour mill? But that does not look like the waterfall at all. The falls are long and narrow. This is far too wide."

"Yes, but this was drawn sixty-nine years ago, before the falls were diverted for the mills. Old timers will tell you the falls used to be wider and more powerful!"

George stuck his face closer to the map. "Okay, mon ami, but how do you explain this? If these are not trees, the arrows point into the falls, then. How can that be? There is nothing but rocks behind the waterfall. You can even see them sticking out."

John nodded. "I know. It's odd." He chewed his lip. "Come on."

"And," continued George chasing after him, "if the falls were wide like that sixty-nine years ago, why did Monsieur Thacker not look there?"

"Maybe he never thought this looked liked a waterfall? I didn't either, until I noticed the map upside down. Then it seemed like those lines might look like moving water."

As they moved diagonally up the mountain, George reached out for a thick tree root to help anchor himself. Before he could react, a hand grabbed George's wrist. A heavyset boy emerged from behind a maple tree.

"Gotcha," said a familiar voice.

"John!" George shouted.

John whirled around and saw Owen holding George in a bear hug.

Chapter 25

Imagine What We Could Become

"Let him go, Owen!" said John.

"Or what?" asked Owen. "You think you're tough now, Johnny, after your time at the lake? Everyone knew that…thing wasn't real."

"Is that why you ran from the old tree the other night when you saw it – after knocking us in the water?"

"George and I have unfinished things to deal with, right George?" he said, ignoring John.

"If you leave him alone you can come with us," John blurted.

"No way, John!" said George. "Do not say it – I am not afraid of him." Owen squeezed harder. "Well, maybe a little," he gasped.

"Why would I want to come with you two any-where?" Owen sneered.

"Because old Mr. Thacker gave us a treasure map. And George and I think we've figured out where it is," said John. He waved it from where he was standing.

Owen lessened his hold and stared at the map.

"You can have ten percent of whatever we find," added John. "But only if you let George go and then don't bother us again."

"Uh, make it fifty," said Owen.

"Okay, you can have fifty percent of the first ten percent that we find," said John. "And that will be one hundred percent of all that you're going to get, okay?"

John could see Owen's brain was starting to hurt from thinking. But he was already releasing his hold on George. "Fine – that's more like it," he said.

John bit his tongue so he wouldn't laugh and mustered a serious expression. "Owen, you are far cleverer than you look." Owen nodded solemnly.

"Now," said John, "let's get going." John, George and Owen moved along the steep hill. The sound of the thick thread of water was a constant as they moved toward the waterfall. The great hill was especially steep here. The falls themselves could be reached by a narrow path along the face of the cliff. The three moved carefully, using coarse roots and embedded rocks to grip along the way.

"John," said George whispering, "I cannot believe we are bringing Owen on what is supposed to be our treasure search."

"It was either that or let Owen take you apart," said John. He glanced back and saw Owen's complexion was green. "Maybe he won't make it anyway," said John. He cupped his hand so Owen could hear. "Something wrong, Owen?"

"Of course not," he said. His voice sounded higher than usual. "Where are you two going, anyway?"

"To the falls," said John.

The waterfall was one hundred-and-fifty-feet above the village. John glanced down a few times and could see a few people moving about the village, but only through the filter of tree branches. No one was looking up that high and John was thankful since adults usually took a dim view of kids near the falls. The end of the narrow path led to an expanded, level area where they had a sparse amount of room to stand near the falls. The spray from the thread of water misted John's face as he found his footing on the ledge. George and Owen joined him.

"It's really slippery up here from the water," warned John. "We better be – whoa!"

George reached out and steadied John who crouched lower until his heart slowed some. "Are you alright, mon ami?"

John nodded. "See?" said George, pointing to the rocks that jutted out from both sides of the falls. "It does not make any sense. Nothing is here."

John crept closer and pulled at some of the smaller rocks that were sticking out of the back of the falls.

"George – these are loose!" He pulled it out and was careful to set it on the expanse of ledge, rather than have it tumble down the great hill and hit the mill or another building.

"Give me a hand – but make sure we pile all the rocks here. We don't want them to fall down the mountain."

Owen and George joined John, carefully piling all of the rocks they were removing. Owen was able to carry twice as much as John and George. As they removed the rocks from behind the falls, it was obvious that the space behind the waterfall was opening up into something larger.

"This is turning into some sort of cave," said John. He was breathing more heavily now from the work and he couldn't have been more elated. George hadn't even checked his hair in twenty minutes, John realized, since he was so excited. Of course, it looked the same as always.

"John, you must have been right. There is going to be room here to have hidden something!"

Owen scrunched his forehead as he moved his muscled arms with greater speed. "I hope it's gold. Remember how much I get, you two."

"Oh, we won't forget," said John. He rolled his eyes at George when Owen wasn't looking. After Owen moved a particularly large rock they could see open space.

"It is a cave!" said John. They worked quickly until there was a crawl space big enough to peer into. "George, can you fit in there?" asked John. "You're the smallest."

His friend looked at the dark hole and swallowed. John knew he was weighing the discovery of treasure with the unknown. He didn't blame him.

"I'll try." George pointed both of his arms as if he were diving and started to push himself through the opening. John steadied George's legs as he belly-crawled over the rocks. "Hey, I think I'm stuck," he said wriggling his torso to try and fit through.

"No problem," said Owen. He grabbed both of George's ankles and shoved hard. The boy disappeared through the hole.

"Oww!"

John heard him say something additional in French that he didn't quite understand. "George, we can't quite hear you."

"I was just talking to Owen."

Owen scowled. "I don't speak French."

"I know," said George. "Hey, John!" he added, his voice muffled by the cave. "I cannot see anything in here. It is damp…really dark. Keep moving stones. I will do the same thing from this side."

Owen and John moved quickly from the outside while George removed rocks toward himself on the inside of the cave. Soon they were able to open up an increasingly larger space. John was able to squeeze his lanky frame through easily now while Owen forced his oversized body to comply, crashing through the other side. A few small stones went over the side and John prayed that no one noticed.

Once inside, John realized the cave itself was about the size of a small room. The waterfall continued to cascade toward the mill below, overshooting the mouth of the cave.

"This is fantastic," said John. "There must have been a small avalanche of some kind which sealed it." He looked around in the dim light.

"There's nothing here," said Owen. He was now at the far end of the cave and wore a look of disgust. John and George looked around, touching the walls and feeling the ground with their hands as if another room would appear somehow.

"I don't understand," said John. He wiped his forehead with the back of his arm because his hands were blackened from the dirt. "I just know this is the place. I can feel it."

Owen shifted his weight quickly toward John and George, who backed up against the wall. "You know what I feel? That you two are a waste of my time."

John stopped breathing for a moment to guard against Owen's breath. "We're going to keep looking," said John.

"And once we find it, you'll still get your share," said George.

Owen snorted then appeared to consider things. "That's right. Anything you two find is fifty percent mine."

"You mean fifty percent of the first ten percent that we find," said John. "Remember, that represents one hundred percent of all that you're going to get. Yes – you have our word on it."

"Whatever," said Owen, already turning. "I'm going home."

John and George looked at one another with a sigh of relief. They peered outside after a couple of minutes and saw Owen lumbering down the side of the mountain. George leaned back, dejected. "It was a great idea, John. Too bad there is nothing here."

John leaned back and felt the soft earth of the floor of the cave. He used his heel to rub the dirt where he saw some discolouration. The small brown patch grew larger as he rubbed and he soon realized it was something buried just beneath the surface.

"What's this?" He reached out and gently pulled on the brown material. It was soft and supple. A rectangular shaped leather pouch was in his hand. John brushed most of the dirt from it and scuttled to the mouth of the cave where there was more light. George joined him.

"What's inside? Gem stones?"

"Too light for that," said John. He reached in and gently pulled out a single letter. The surface of the paper was similar to the treasure map. Carefully, he unfolded it and stared. "George, it's in French!" said John. "And look, there's a year at the top – 1759!"

"That's the year Monsieur Thacker said it was – and that it was a French admiral who gave him the map!" added George.

John handed it over. "Come on, read it. I can only pick out certain words – and don't leave anything out."

George took the letter and skimmed over the contents so he could understand what he was reading and to familiarize himself with the man's handwriting. He swallowed. Even in the dim light of the cave John read the unease in his friend's eyes.

George read.

September 30, 1759

Dear Annette,

Let this not be my last letter to you, I pray. Earlier today, I received word that General Wolfe has defeated General Montcalm in Quebec. Both are dead. Quebec has fallen, although I am certain other battles will go on.

I have found an incredible, room-sized cave behind the waterfall on the mountain I earlier described. From my vantage point here, one hundred and fifty feet above, I can see British ships in the distance. With a heavy heart I realize a pitched sea battle is about to begin. Some other British ships, I fear, have already landed quietly, bringing soldiers to this strategic area.

And yet I must return to my ship, Annette, to rejoin my men. It will not be easy for it is a long and treacherous open shoreline. Pray for me that I make it. I have already sketched a rough map to this cave which I will bring with me, since I am unsure of when I might be able to return.

I have a small bounty on board my ship that I have been saving, which I will also hide in this cave when I return. If I am not successful in my return, then only this final letter shall remain here. All that I have saved on board may then be lost to the ages. A sailor's salary is no great fortune, even for one recently named 'admiral.' But it would be a start for us.

Truly, the treasure I have always sought is here, Annette, but only with you beside me. It seems a shame to continue to fight over this land, my love, for the more I see of the size and scope of it there is room enough for all. Perhaps I am too old for hatred now, but I grow weary of this war and wish others were also this tired. If each side were to turn their cannons down, imagine what we could build, here in this untamed land!

Imagine what a nation we could become.

But that is not for one admiral to decide, is it? Perhaps one day someone will stumble upon these words, or words like them, and find such a path to take. I leave these thoughts here in the hope that I may one day read them to you aloud in what would become our new country...our new home. Yet one way or another, I shall see you again.

Yours Now and Forevermore,

Joseph

Chapter 26

The Truth of it All

With both hands on the thick, wooden handle, John heaved the largest suitcase in front of him towards the bay where Cornelius would arrive this morning. George trailed with a smaller piece of luggage. Both contained John's life in Kingston, until he would return again next year. The last couple of days had gone by quickly.

"You're sure you're okay with me keeping the letter?" asked John as they stumbled along.

"Oui, I am sure. Besides, it will help your French," said George and grinned. "Guess what? Father tells me I might be able to visit you in Kingston, if we go this fall for supplies. We can look for serpents in Lake Ontario."

John stopped and set the suitcase down so he could hit George in the arm.

"Oww!"

"Don't even think about it," said John. As he continued walking, John looked down the strip of sand and water of the Bay of Quinte. To think that the French admiral had died here only a few feet away from where they stood captivated John. He looked down the edge of the bay and pictured the dying admiral reaching out and stuffing the rough sketch of map into the hands of the only person he could see. And to think that same young person was Jeremiah Thacker, now an old man, gave John a chill.

"Great," said George, glancing over his shoulder. "Here comes your little sister again. Why does she always have to mess up my hair?"

"Like Moll said, she likes you," said John, laughing.

"Mon dieu," muttered George. He avoided Lou by speeding ahead to chat with Solomon Brook.

"Are you sad, John?" asked Lou, as she and Moll caught up with John.

"Some," said John. "Kingston's always a great adventure too – even with school. But I'll miss you all, that's for sure."

"John?" said Lou.

"Yes?"

"Thank you for coming to get me out on the lake."

"You're welcome Lou – you already thanked me you know."

She shrugged. "I know." She took off to chase George.

Nearly at the shore, John gratefully set the oversized

suitcase down and then sat on it. Its hard wooden sides easily accommodated his tall, lean frame. Moll joined him. She gave her brother a quick hug around his shoulder.

"Moll?"

"Hmm."

"Remember when we were playing chess a few days ago?"

"Yes."

"And you said I'm the only one carrying James inside of me with that memory – because I was the only one there?" She nodded.

"I don't want that to be the only thought I have of James."

"I don't blame you."

"When I let go of that memory – even a bit – I start to remember other things about him. Better things." Moll hugged him again and John could see her pale skin was blotched with pink. "You'll write?" Moll asked.

"Of course."

"You'll get better at chess?" John shoved her a little and she laughed.

"In chess, the colonel shows no mercy," said John. "Every game is like reliving a war for him. Guess I'll have to get better if I want to win any matches at all." He squinted toward the bay. "Well, there's Cornelius."

The long, slender *Morning Bloom* glided to shore and

John could see the blonde, unkempt hair of Cornelius blowing in the breeze. John noticed Solomon Brook making his way over, too.

"Where's Mother – and Father?" John asked Moll.

"They're coming," said Moll. "Mother's packing you and Cornelius something to eat. She'll bring Father down from the mill."

A moment later they saw their mother exit the house with a basket and then enter the flour mill. Hugh brushed off flour from his pants as he walked beside Helen toward the shoreline. Cornelius was just loosely tying the bateau, when they arrived to where John and Moll were sitting.

The bateau operator quickly began loading other cargo that farmers and traders had brought this morning while the Macdonald's said their goodbyes.

"So this is it again?" asked Hugh, smiling. "Stay well, son." He offered his hand and John shook it. His father gave him half of an uncertain hug. "I can't stay long – got to get back to the mill with business picking up."

"It's great that it's getting busy, again, Father," said John, watching another wagon pull up. "Stay well, too."

Helen asked four or five rapid questions – John lost count – about everything that he had packed. Once she was satisfied, she hugged him tightly. "You concentrate on your school work, you hear?"

"Yes, Mother."

She grabbed him gently by the arm and steered him off to one side.

Oh no. Now what?

"The last time your father was in Kingston he stopped in to chat with George Mackenzie."

"The lawyer?" asked John.

"That's right. He's a young one, but a real up-and-comer. He told your father if your marks are good you could start working with him when you turn fifteen."

John smiled and glanced at the others. "Are you serious, Mother? Really?"

"Yes, really. Now listen, the family's depending on you, John. You might not realize it yet, but we'll need you. This is an important path for you." She grabbed John's curly head and kissed him on the cheek and then handed him the food basket. "You'll share with Cornelius?"

"Of course."

Cornelius overheard this part and tipped an imaginary hat toward Helen in thanks. Then he lugged the two suitcases on board and stored them with other cargo.

"Careful, lad!" said Solomon. "That first suitcase alone will likely sink that thing long before Kingston."

"Only if you're coming along with it," said Cornelius. Solomon laughed while his large belly shook.

After a few more brief hugs and warm wishes from everyone John boarded the bateau and Cornelius gently eased the boat out into the Bay of Quinte. John stood at the bow and waved.

As his family and friends grew smaller, he thought about how his future was growing in ways he could not have imagined at the start of summer. In only a year and a half he could be working as an apprenticing lawyer in Kingston. It was hard to feel the exact shape of his future – but maybe this was the right place to start.

John sat back against his luggage and listened to the water beneath them. He gazed at the cornflower blue of the sky creeping by, content with the gentle sounds of the lake beneath them. Cornelius was in a quiet mood and that suited John fine.

His gaze shifted to the brooding pine trees on his left. The bateau moved forward and then past a stretch of open sand fifteen miles east of Stone Mills. He squinted at the shore and saw a small cooking fire. An old man with a long, grey beard was stirring something in a metal pot over the fire.

Jeremiah Thacker!

"Cornelius, can we please stop there, near that man," said John, pointing to the figure on the sand. "Please, it's very important – I can't really explain quickly. You don't even have to tie up the boat."

Cornelius pulled out a bronze pocket watch. "Ten

minutes, John. That's it."

John waved to Jeremiah Thacker from the bateau. The old man waved back, uncertainly. Cornelius moved closer to the shoreline and John rolled his pant legs above his knees. Then he grabbed a long crust of bread from the food basket and stuffed it inside one of his vest pockets. The other pocket contained the letter written by Admiral Fortin sixty-nine years ago – the same man who had thrust the letter into a young Jeremiah Thacker's hand when he was a young boy.

When the water was suitably shallow, John jumped over the side and landed on his bare feet. He ran to shore while Cornelius held the bateau steady. As he sloshed onto the shore, Jeremiah met him half way. John couldn't wait to tell him they had solved the location of the treasure map in less than two weeks.

He's going to be so excited.

"Well good day, young man. Been thinkin' about you. Headin' off to Kingston?"

"Yes, sir…I have to resume my schooling."

"The bay's been busy," said Jeremiah, "what with all that serpent nonsense. Ran into a farmer yesterday who told me 'bout the American soldiers. Fact is, he heard it was you who played a big part in that."

John smiled and nodded. He thought he was going to burst if he didn't tell the old man the news about the hidden cave.

"Well, good for you," said Jeremiah. "Come and sit down on old Jeremiah's driftwood for a minute." They both sat down on the old partial tree that had washed ashore.

"Say, do you have time for a little muskrat soup while you're here? Might be a little thin this time – it's the second time I've used the bones."

John's stomach heaved. "Thank you, but I have to be getting back with Cornelius," said John, gesturing to the bateau. "Mr. Thacker, I just –"

"Listen, before you say anythin' I want to apologize," said Jeremiah. "It was unfair for me to do that to you, givin' you that map and all. I meant well – but expectin' a few young ones to find something that took up my entire life, well…that wasn't a nice thing for me to do."

"But Mr. Thacker we actually – "

"And then I got to thinkin,' you know what might even be worse?"

John shook his head.

"What if you were able to find it quickly – what kind of a feeble brain would I be then, huh?" He laughed and shook his head. John winced.

"And who knows – what if there was no treasure at all?" the old man continued. "After all this time of nothin' but thinkin' about it! What if there was no treasure to be found?"

John laughed uneasily and stared at his feet. Jeremiah

picked up a stick and poked at his fire. "Some days I think I might have imagined that French admiral who died in front of me. Sure, I had the map. So he must have been real. But some days, he just didn't seem real enough to me."

The old man turned and looked off toward Stone Mills. John felt the crinkle of the letter in his vest pocket, written by Admiral Fortin long ago.

"Now what was it you wanted to tell me, young man? Don't tell me you found the treasure already." Jeremiah laughed and John laughed with him.

Then John reached into his inside vest pocket and hesitated. He pulled out the crust of bread.

"No, sir – we've no idea about that map. I just wanted to give you this. I wasn't sure how much luck you might have had in getting by lately."

The old man took the bread and smiled through his missing teeth. He put a kind hand on John's shoulder and they both stood. The grey-bearded man hugged John. "You're a good lad, you are. Kingston's a lucky town to have you."

"Thank you, sir." John trudged back through the water to the boat and Cornelius extended his hand to help him back on board.

"What was that all about?" Cornelius asked.

John watched the old man eating as he waved from the shore. "Cornelius, what's more important – doing the right thing or telling the truth?"

The boatman thought about it for a moment as he aimed the bateau's nose for Kingston. "Maybe doing the right thing has its own truth."

John nodded as they watched the morning unfold.

Wilfrid LAURIER
on the death of Sir John A. Macdonald

"...the place of Sir John Macdonald in this country was so large and so absorbing that it is almost impossible to conceive that the political life of this country, the fate of this country, can continue without him. His loss overwhelms us. For my part, I say with all truth his loss overwhelms me...as if indeed one of the institutions of the land had given way. Sir John Macdonald now belongs to the ages, and it can be said with certainty that the career which has just been closed is one of the most remarkable careers of this century ... As to his statesmanship, it is written in the history of Canada. It may be said without any exaggeration whatever, that the life of Sir John Macdonald, from the time he entered Parliament, is the history of Canada..."

About the AUTHOR

Roderick Benns was the odd kid in class who had memorized all of the prime ministers in order. Born in Peterborough, Ontario and raised in nearby Lindsay, he has enjoyed a varied writing career spanning more than twenty years, with newspapers, magazines, Internet news sites and radio.

An award-winning journalist, Roderick captured a first place national newspaper award in the 1990s for journalistic initiative through the CCNA.

As owner of Fireside Publishing House, Roderick chose to kick-start the Leaders & Legacies Series with its first two books – the award-winning Mystery of the Moonlight Murder: *An Early Adventure of John Diefenbaker*, and The Legends of Lake on the Mountain: *An Early Adventure of John A. Macdonald*.

Roderick is also Senior Writer with the Literacy and Numeracy Secretariat of the Ontario Ministry of Education.

Family life is integral to Roderick. He is married to Joli Scheidler-Benns, who serves as the Leaders & Legacies Series editor. Roderick has two wonderful children, Eric and Alexis. They live in the Greater Toronto Area with their silver toy poodle, Sirius. The family also likes to spend time in the country with their young horse, Gaelin.

Author VISITS

Roderick is available to speak to your class or service club on any of Canada's prime ministers and Canadian history topics in general. In the classroom, he has a strong understanding of curricular and cross-curricular priorities and can work with teachers to cover the angles needed in presentations.

For your service club, Roderick focuses on Citizenship, Leadership and Canada's Prime Ministers.

Fiction or FACT?

The Legends of Lake on the Mountain:
An Early Adventure of John A. Macdonald

Don't read on if you haven't read the book yet!

Spoiler Alert!

This is a book which imagines an adventure about our greatest founding father, Sir John A. Macdonald. However, there is ample historical truth in here as well. While all ages will hopefully enjoy the adventure, it should also provide a suitable launch point for rich discussions about early Canada, the War of 1812, the Rebellions of 1837, the Seven Years War, responsible government, citizenship, perseverance, and, of course, the destiny and life's work of Sir John A. Macdonald.

Macdonald was instrumental in bringing Canada West (Ontario) and Canada East (Quebec), as well as Nova Scotia, and New Brunswick together in 1867 to form Canada. He would soon after also negotiate British Columbia, PEI, and the vast North West Territories into the national fold. Macdonald was also the driving force behind the Trans-Canadian railway (the longest in the world). He was adept at handling relations with the United States during its expansionist phase and his ability to balance French and English interests was formidable. Macdonald also had to confront the challenge of the Northwest rebellion and created the North West

Mounted Police, forerunner of the Royal Canadian Mounted Police.

Events and truths within this book

I have attempted to render Macdonald's personality in youth from various anecdotes gathered over the years, while also keeping in mind the adult personality for which there is more of a public record. It is my hope you will have found the fun-loving, ambitious, emotionally-intelligent man we know from history within these pages.

The opening scene of this book was borrowed and adapted from a story E.B. Biggar tells about a young John A., who "aroused the displeasure of one of his companions."

"The aggrieved boy, who was larger than he, caught Johnny in the flour mill, and having laid him prostrate, proceeded to rub flour into the jet locks of his hair until it was quite white."

This formed the basis for the Owen Boggart flour incident which opened the first scene.

John A.'s dreams about being in a Kingston tavern with his little brother were true, overall. We know that John's younger brother, James, was struck by a man named Kennedy, who was an employee of Hugh Macdonald's at the time. James died from this incident while John watched helplessly.

George Cloutier was meant to symbolically represent George Étienne-Cartier, one of our most important fathers of Confederation, along with Macdonald. He became a close friend of Macdonald's later in life. Since they didn't actually grow up together, I could not include the real Cartier. However, I thought it was important to hint at the importance of the man who had helped Macdonald guide Quebec into Confederation.

The idea that a French admiral hid his treasure somewhere in the Glenora (Stone Mills) area in a cave is a famous local legend from Prince Edward County. I took liberties to explain how this French admiral may have come to the area and what his intent for his treasure was. I weaved the storyline to hint at a vision of a united Canada.

The lake serpent of Lake on the Mountain is also culled from local myth. For more information on these and many other legends in Prince Edward County, the author recommends *The Legendary Guide to Prince Edward County* by Janet Kellough.

Everything about John's family was rendered as truthfully as possible based on available research, including Lieutenant Colonel Donald Macpherson. The reader may wonder why Lieutenant Colonel Donald Macpherson's name was sometimes written as 'Colonel Macpherson' and sometimes 'Lieutenant Colonel Macpherson.' In military tradition, a lieutenant colonel can be "Colonel" in conversation. In dialogue, everyone spoke of him as Colonel Macpherson or 'the colonel.' But in attribution, his full rank must be spelled out.

In real life, the colonel would become increasingly ill and then die just one year after the events of this book.

The colonel's son, Allan Macpherson, was an entrepreneur who really did live in Napanee. Today, the same Georgian-style mansion exists as a museum called Macpherson House.

The author took liberties with the size of Stone Mills at this time for dramatic effect, rendering it a bit larger then it likely was at this time.

Virtually all names in this book were created through birth and marriage records of the time in Prince Edward County. Instead of using the actual names, the author mixed and matched first and last names to retain the true flavour of the time period and locale without actually using real names, other than historical figures, such as Macdonald and his family.

An exception to this rule was Pastor Macdowell, who was a real pastor in the Hallowell (Picton) area. He came across from the U.S. at the invitation of Peter Van Alstine, who had led many United Empire Loyalists to the Adolphustown area. One other exception was ferryman Jacob Adams, who really did operate the ferry during 1828.

The story of the great drowning in Prince Edward

County is true, including the verse from the actual song which many people memorized and sang, including school children.

History tells us that Kingston actually was in the middle of a typhoid outbreak when the colonel visits the Macdonald's.

The author found several conflicting sources on just when Hugh Macdonald, John's father, moved from Hay Bay to Stone Mills (or present-day Glenora). The age in which John A was said to have moved to Stone Mills ranged from 10 to 14. The author chose the age 13 for the storyline and references John having lived in the Stone Mills area "for a couple of years" to reflect the vagueness surrounding this move from Hay Bay.

More well documented is the fact that John A. Macdonald was articled to a young Scottish lawyer, George Mackenzie, of Kingston, in 1830. Later that same year he went to York (Toronto) to appear before the Law Society. Following the exam, he was given his law certificate and formally admitted to the society as a student at law. He opened his own law office in Kingston on August 24, 1835.

– Roderick Benns

**Bellevue House National Historic Site
is located in Kingston, Ontario, and is a short drive
from Sir John A.'s childhood home in Glenora.**

Now owned and operated by Parks Canada, Bellevue House was home to John A. Macdonald and his young family in 1848-49. Already a successful lawyer, Macdonald lived at Bellevue House while balancing his law practice, political ambitions and the needs of his ill wife and young son.

Today, Bellevue House National Historic site welcomes thousands of visitors every year. The house has been restored to the 1840's time period, so you can experience what life was like for John A. The site also includes enlightening exhibits, a multi-lingual video, historic gardens and knowledgeable staff who delight in sharing their favourite stories about Sir John A. Macdonald.

For more information including rates, hours of operation, curriculum based learning programs and special events, visit us on the web:

www.pc.gc.ca/bellevue

Areas for Further STUDY

The Family Compact

The Family Compact was the unofficial name of the small group of individuals in Upper Canadian political life who were more properly called Tories. They were the local elite and occupied positions such as administrators, businessmen, judiciary, clergy, landowners and lawyers in the 1820s and 1830s.

The fact that the commercial and personal interests of the Family Compact were put ahead of the interests of the people of the colony was a key reason for the Rebellions of 1837.

The Loyalists

When the U.S. decisively severed its ties with Britain through a bloody revolution, this had a cascade effect in many ways. For pre-Confederation Canada, it literally meant rewriting our very boundaries for the great influx of people who wanted to continue living under the British umbrella.

By 1783, thousands of Loyalists left the newly-created United States. Most set their course for Nova Scotia, as well as the unused lands above the St. Lawrence rapids and north of Lake Ontario. Such a massive influx of settlers was effectively the first real wave of immigrants by English-speaking settlers. It was so large, in fact, that their arrival had immediate consequences for the British colonies.

Nova Scotia and the inland colony of Quebec had to be reorganized to reflect these new realities. At this time, Nova Scotia included the wild forests to the west of the Bay of Fundy. In 1784, this area was established as a separate colony known as New Brunswick. In total, about 35,000 Loyalist immigrants settled in Canada's Maritimes.

Another sizable group of about 5,000 United Empire Loyalists chose land north and west of Lake Ontario and along the north shore of the upper St. Lawrence. This included the watery inlets and reaches of Prince Edward County, where a young John A. Macdonald once lived with his family.

The Durham Report

One of the most important reports ever written in British history occurred less than ten years after the timeline of this book. Queen Victoria, new to the throne in 1837, was worried that her North American colonies would crumble without British intervention. The Rebellions of 1837 had just occurred, in large part because of Family Compact policies. She soon requested that John Lambton, the earl of Durham, analyze what was wrong in Upper and Lower Canada. Upper and Lower Canada had many challenges during the early 19th century. Both colonies contained political cliques, like the Family Compact, and both existed under anti-democratic conditions.

Lord Durham arrived in the spring of 1838 and after much investigation he made three key recommendations. They were:

• responsible government should be granted to the British North American colonies
• Upper and Lower Canada should be amalgamated to form a united Province of Canada
• French Canadians should be assimilated

The last of his recommendations was obviously the most controversial. It was the 'fatal flaw' in terms of gaining widespread acceptance and political support. The report was certainly reviled by French Canadians and even to this day, it is this last recommendation that continues to be remembered the most.

Yet the Durham Report's first two important recommendations would come to pass and were important evolutionary milestones in the nation's development. Durham recommended that Upper and Lower Canada be united with a single parliament. He noted that freer colonies would create more loyalty to the Mother country, not less. They just had to be given the freedom to do so. Lord Durham even went so far as to predict the notion of a union, one day, of all the British colonies in North America.

The people of Lower Canada resisted so strongly that in 1848, seven years after the Act of Union was passed, England was forced to formally recognize and accept the use of French.

Lord Durham, in missing the mark so clearly with his recommendation to assimilate the French, had made a fatal error. It was an error that the country's future founder – and subject of this book – would never have made. Throughout his entire life, John A. Macdonald urged English-speaking Conservatives to work in partnership with French Canadians.

"Treat them as a nation and they will act as a free people generally do – generously. Call them a faction, and they become factious."

– John A. Macdonald

Manifest Destiny

This was an unofficial government policy in 1800's America. Manifest destiny referred to a widely-held belief by many Americans at the time that the U.S. was destined to rule over the entire North American continent.

Technically, this term was not yet around during the events of this book. However, the idea of 'continentalism' was, which was a precursor to manifest destiny. The term manifest destiny did actually not get used until the 1840s. An early proponent of continentalism was President John Quincy Adams, to whom the character Darius Marshall refers to in this book.

Books and Sources Used in Writing This Book

Biggar, E.B. *Anecdotal Life of Sir John Macdonald*; Montreal, John Lovell & Son; 1891.

Creighton, Donald. *John A. Macdonald: The Young Politician. The Old Chieftain*; Toronto, University of Toronto Press; 1952.

County Magazine, Issue Numbers 19, 101 and 102.

Gwyn, Richard. *John A: The Man Who Made Us*; Toronto, Random House Canada; 2007.

Napanee Beaver, *'The Great Drowning,'* April 30, 1897 edition.

Phenix, Patricia. *Private Demons: The Tragic Personal Life of John A. Macdonald*; Toronto, McClelland & Stewart; 2006.

Pope, Joseph. *Memoirs of the Right Honourable Sir John Alexander Macdonald First Prime Minister of the Dominion of Canada*, Ottawa; 1894.

Sewell, John. *Mackenzie: A Political Biography of William Lyon Mackenzie*; Toronto, J. Lorimer & Co; 2002.

Miss the award-winning Book One in the *Leaders & Legacies Series*?

Murder and mystery on the Canadian prairies!

August, 1908. One hundred years ago, under the light of a full moon, 12-year-old John Diefenbaker and his younger brother, Elmer, are nearby when their neighbour is shot to death in a field. The murder in small-town Saskatchewan ignites a desperate search for the killer by the Royal North West Mounted Police.

When a family friend of the Diefenbakers is arrested for the murder, a man from a Plains Cree band, John is certain they have the wrong person. With the help of the man's 11-year-old daughter, Summer Storm, John and Elmer set out to prove his innocence. But with only five days left before the murder trial, time is running out.

Meanwhile a charismatic Metis man named Andre Dumont, claiming to be related to the famous military commander Gabriel Dumont, is trying to stir up anger against the federal government. The last thing the police need is another full-scale rebellion on their hands.

From a smooth-talking Rawleigh's salesman, to a testy general store owner, to mysterious strangers...all is not what it seems. See how these colourful characters not only challenged the Canadian west but also the sense of justice and fairness in a young boy who would one day lead the nation.

Buy the first book in the series at www.firesidepublishinghouse.com for your children, grandchildren or another young person you know.

Spread the Word!

Consider giving this book as a gift

• Buy a copy of this book at firesidepublishinghouse.com for your children, grandchildren or as a gift idea. When you buy from Fireside, each book is personally signed by the author.

• If you have a website or blog, consider sharing your thoughts about the idea of the Leaders & Legacies series. Canada needs more voices to support our national identity, our national stories

• Write a book review for your local newspaper or for a favourite website. Contact your favourite radio show to suggest the author as a future guest.

• Store and business owners — consider putting a small display of this book on your counter or in some other available space. We offer discount pricing for purchasing five or more books.

• Contact the author and have him speak to your group, class or service club.

Support Canada's
Leaders & Legacies series

Free STUFF

• Download the first three chapters of The Mystery of the Moonlight Murder: *An Early Adventure of John Diefenbaker*

• Listen to the author read Chapter One of The Mystery of the Moonlight Murder: *An Early Adventure of John Diefenbaker*

• Sign up for the monthly newsletter *The Canadian* – the newsletter of Canadian history (see next page for more information)

• Download our Prime Ministers' Cheat Sheet. Lists every prime minister and two accomplishments each!

• Download Five Tips on teaching with historical fiction

All at www.roderickbenns.com

Subscribe to *The CANADIAN*

Log onto www.roderickbenns.com and fill out the form with your name and email address to subscribe to the free monthly newsletter, *The Canadian,* produced by Roderick Benns.

This dynamic newsletter brings history alive and focuses on history news, as well as history topics, such as the Prime Ministers, Confederation, Métis and First Nations settlers, early Canada, Canadian-American relations, the Federal government, the development of Western Canada, the role of the Canadian Pacific Railway, the North-West Rebellion and the role of Gabriel Dumont and Louis Riel, the RCMP, its role and early mandate, citizenship, the War of 1812, the Rebellion of 1837, Responsible Government and the Durham Report, United Empire Loyalists and more! These are topics generally covered in Social Studies and History provincial curricula from Grades 4 through Grade 9.

All at www.roderickbenns.com

Questions & ANSWERS

Q: Isn't a novel just a novel? How will this attract more students to reading, especially boys?

A: Some experts point out that nearly 50 percent of boys describe themselves as non-readers by the time they enter secondary school. That's a real problem. Part of the issue in elementary school and middle school is that we know a book's content is very relevant for boys as a motivator. So in many cases, it is not that boys do not like to read, but that they do not like to read what they are presented with in the classroom. Boys like to read books that reflect what they aspire to be, or to do. They want reading that appeals to their sense of mischief. They want action – not an over-emphasis on the emotions. They also love books in series, likely because there is comfort in familiarity. The Leaders & Legacies series brings all of these elements to the forefront.

Q: What about girls? Will they be inclined to enjoy this series?

A. Absolutely! The thing about girls is they tend to have more flexible reading habits, overall. Many girls will resonate with the themes in these books, and we know they tend to appreciate strong characters and character development overall. As much as we have suspense and action, which girls like as well, we also have multi-faceted storylines. There are great female characters in all of our books.

Q. Are you saying students will actually learn more when taught using historical fiction than if they were using a traditional text book?

A. Yes and no. A historical fiction offering is meant to be a companion to a history book – it is a great entry point for key learning and discussions guided by the teacher.

However there was a 1992 study by Guzzetti, Kowalinski and McGowan who demonstrated that the Grade Six kids they studied actually absorbed more social studies concepts when they were taught through literature instead of a text book. They felt this was because stories helped to clarify ideas for kids since people of this age tend to personalize things more.

So if there is a way we can provide an enriched entry point into Canadian history for kids – and we think this is a key role for historical fiction – then we must measure this as a success.

Q: Is there a reason parents, too, will be especially involved in guiding their kids to read this book and this series?

A: Yes – and I think grandparents, too. It is so important to have parents involved in their children's reading and this series, in particular, should be of high interest to anyone who feels we need to do more to encourage a connection between young people and their country. We are also very excited about public libraries and school libraries getting involved to help us share with a broader audience of students.

Q: Why give so much attention to Canada's leaders?

A: One of the things we think Canada would benefit from would be to create more of a culture of respect between citizens and leaders, and leaders to leaders. Americans do this very well. There is a genuine respect for the office of the presidency which transcends the individuals who hold it.

Our Prime Ministers (and other Canadian 'leaders') are people who provide living evidence of personal sacrifice, service to country, and, yes, ambition. From our stand-point, we want children to know this is possible for them. We want them to know that serving one's country will not invite ridicule or disdain but rather respect and appreciation, assuming their intent is in the best interests of their fellow Canadians.

Q. What is your overall hope for this series, aside from strong book sales?

A. We hope this will become a movement. We hope that the Leaders & Legacies series will serve to inspire all Canadians. If it sparks and sustains a deeper love for Canada then we will have accomplished a great deal together.